Acclaim for *A Woman of Means* and Peter Taylor

"No one writes more beautifully than Peter Taylor of the tensions of love."
—Joyce Carol Oates, *The Southern Review*

"Peter Taylor's been writing about middle-class America for years, yet most of us are unfamiliar with his work. He's an exceptional short story writer, but it's his novel, *A Woman of Means*, that we want to call to your attention. The story of a boy who witnesses his family's unravelling, this is a book full of secrets, and it's bound to cast light on a writer whose talent is one of the best secrets of all."
—*Esquire*

"The mood of the novel, which is elegiac, and its style, which is spare and precise, are reminiscent of Willa Cather, and the locale—St. Louis in the mid-twenties—seems as remote in time as Ms. Cather's Nebraska of the mid-nineties."
—*The New Yorker*

"As Taylor often said, a writer is as good as his best work, and the Peter Taylor of *A Woman of Means* and many of his stories is very good indeed. . . . His vision is complete and achieves, I think, its fullest fruition in *A Woman of Means*."
—Walter Sullivan, *The Sewanee Review*

"It is characteristic of Taylor that his theme is developed not through the narrator's triumphs but through his failures. There is little room in Taylor's fiction for heroes. Most of his people, like most of the world's, live not in dreams, but in reality. No doubt that is one reason why, to those of us who so greatly admire and love his fiction, it cuts so close to home."
—Jonathan Yardley, *The Washington Post Book World*

Peter Taylor   A Woman of Means

Peter Taylor

A Woman of Means

Picador USA
New York

Picador® is a U.S. registered trademark and is used by St.
Martin's Press under license from Pan Books Limited.

Library of Congress Cataloging-in-Publication Data

Taylor, Peter Hillsman
        A woman of means / by Peter Taylor.
            p.   cm.
        ISBN 0-312-14448-2
            1. Married people—Missouri—Saint Louis—Fiction.
    2. Fathers and sons—Missouri—Saint Louis—Fiction.   3.
    Stepmothers—Missouri—Saint Louis—Fiction.   I. Title.
    PS3539.A9633W6   1996
    813'.54—dc20   96-4261
                                                          CIP

First published in the United States of America by Frederic C.
Beil, Publisher

First Picador USA Edition: August 1996

10   9   8   7   6   5   4   3   2   1

For Katherine Baird Taylor

The girls kept diaries, but you never had a chance to read them. They kept them locked away—Laura's in her top bureau drawer, Bess's in the secret compartment of her desk. Diaries, besides, had keys. Laura wore hers on a bracelet with other trinkets—a gold heart and a tiny ivory slipper. Bess kept hers pinned to the black silk lining of her everyday purse or sometimes under the strap of an evening gown.

'Only Diary knows that!' they would say if I asked too many questions.

'I'll ask Diary,' they would say if I asked when something or other happened.

'Diary is a girl's best friend.'

'Pardon me, I've got to go tell Diary something rich.'

'It's just as I was saying to Diary last night: All men are beasts.'

Sometimes they would let me stay in the room while they wrote in Diary and ask me for a man's opinion on something. For instance: 'What do men think of a girl who late-dates?' They would laugh at whatever I answered and twist its meaning till it really seemed to be kind of smutty. If they had been my real sisters I might have asked them outright what they meant, but they were only my stepsisters, and I had always to remember that they were young ladies or soon would be. Laura had a portable phonograph in her room with stickers on it from Bar Harbor and Miami and Catalina Island. Bess had autographed pictures from a dozen movie stars on her wall, and she had souvenir menus from restaurants in New Orleans and one printed in Spanish from Mexico City. They had been everywhere, because they always traveled with their real father in the summertime. There was a picture of him on Laura's vanity taken at Palm Beach with his new wife, whom they called the Madam. Bess collected pillows. For footstools she had two square pillows covered with black oilcloth and spotted with dice marks. Laura had a shelf of china dogs. If there had only been a chance to read their diaries! but there never was.

Sometimes Father played rotation pool in the billiard room with his new stepdaughters and me. The billiard room was the only room in my stepmother's great house where he seemed to have taken possession. Soon after they were married he had had the table cushions rebuilt and a new baize cover put on. The workmen delivered the new cushions late one afternoon when I was sitting alone in the library. I looked up from the afternoon funny-paper just in time to see the cushions being carried through the dark hallway. They were wrapped in white sheeting, and as I saw them being borne through the hall on the shoulders of the men, I momentarily mistook the cushions for a corpse, because at that time I was forever anticipating accidental death for some member of the family (by auto or streetcar collision, or by the fall of an elevator), and a hideous gurgling sound came from my throat. Afterward I felt so foolish that I did not speak of it even to my stepmother, whom I adored and in whom I confided nearly everything.

My father had all the cues refinished and retipped, and he ordered a new lighting fixture to go above the table and nearly a hundred bulbs for the indirect lighting in the molding. He had the painters come and put a new coat of white paint on the vaulted ceiling, and he bought a new draw shade for the skylight. In the evenings we played rotation until the girls' dates arrived.

'Where are you going tonight?' I might ask the girls.

'Out,' they would say. 'Just out.' And they would throw me a kiss across the green table or run a hand through my hair. That was the answer they gave me; but if Father asked, they explained their plans in detail. They told their stepfather far more than they told their own mother. 'Billy took me to the Marietta Club last night,' Laura said one night as she stood by the table watching Father sight along his cue. 'But don't you tell Mother, for Lord's sake.' Bess, meanwhile, moved nearer to Father and corrected the angle of his cue, because the girls had been coaching him in this game that he had previously looked down on. They had lured him back to the billiard room, at the time of his courtship with their mother, and taught him the games that their own father had taught them when they were little girls. 'Furthermore,' Laura contined, 'Pep Lewis is taking me back to Marietta's tonight, because tonight I expect to see the second inning of a little game I watched the start of last night.'

Father completed his shot, as usual with little success, then turned his whole attention to his step-daughters. He seemed quite as eager as I for any scraps of enlightenment which the girls would throw out. When Laura and Bess talked about themselves or about the people they saw away from home and about the places they went, his interest in the game receded so perceptibly that I would be annoyed and embarrassed, especially if I had to remind Father that it was his turn to play again.

'What is the little game you spoke about, Laura?'

'Oh, I think it's love in bloom again, dearest one.'

'And who is it this time? You or Bess?'

'Oh, neither of us, Father-chum. Not even in our crowd, but in your crowd.'

'My crowd?'

'Oh yes. Your crowd, m'love.'

'Now go ahead and tell him about it, Laura,' urged Bess, who was the more direct and literal-minded of the two sisters.

'No, you tell him, sugar; you're refined,' Laura said, arching her eyebrows.

'Well, it's Mr. Tom Colby.'

'No, no. It's the young Colby—Bill, you mean.'

'Oh, no. The president of your company! Mr. Colby and one of the girls that sing at Marietta's. Apparently he thinks she's the bee's knees.'

Father put down his cue, blushing.

'It's quite true,' Bess said, 'but you mustn't tell Mother about all this.'

'Your mother knows you go to Marietta's.'

'But she doesn't know what goes on there.'

'What does go on there?' He was trying to show only casual interest. 'I doubt if you girls ought to go to such a place.'

'Oh, everybody goes there.'

'Yes, it's one of the regular places now.'

'It's funny but nobody goes to the Rainbow any more.'

'Not a soul. Nobody.'

When the girls' dates arrived Father would try to get them to stay long enough for a game of rotation. But they never stayed. There was usually someone waiting in the car. If the girls went upstairs to fetch their coats and things, the young men might borrow Father's cue and, calling their shots, prove their excellence in the game that they never had time to play. Then the girls would come down again and kiss their stepfather good night. They would hug him and whisper in his ear, 'You're a sweet thing,' or, 'I love you.'

When they first used to do this his face would redden, and it seemed that he hardly knew where to look. But before many months he grew accustomed to their familiarities and confident of their affection for him. Indeed, before the first year had passed I understood, from half-concealed references, that there were times during my own absence when the girls confided even their closest secrets to my father. Even the bond between my stepmother and me seemed hardly stronger than that between Father and the girls. Finally he assumed with them the same tone of authority that my stepmother already used with me. If Bess sometimes only poked her head in the billiard room before going out—just to signal her date and perhaps to say, 'Father, my mammy's upstairs wanting to know where that man of hers is'—he would complain that she had not kissed him good night, and he might even send her back to put on a heavier coat. For Laura was only seventeen then, and Bess was a year younger.

One night when Laura and Bess had gone out in evening dress (after Father had watched their beaus in tuxedos making several precision shots) he remained a while in the billiard room with me. He took off his coat and in his vest and shirtsleeves was practicing some of the difficult plays. For the first time I noticed his improvement in the game. And at the same time I could not help thinking of days when Father used to say that a pool parlor was the breeding place of ne'er-do-wells. In those days when my father had merely traveled for the hardware company, before he was even a second or third vice-president, his temper had seemed very different—the sight of a man in shirtsleeves would be the occasion for a lecture on gentlemanliness to me. And after those lectures I would retire to some spot in the back hallway of our rooming house, or at another time to a corner of our efficiency apartment, and ponder what my father had said.

But tonight I was trying to decide whether or not Father's physical appearance had changed with his success, when he asked absently: 'What are you thinking, Quint?'

'You've improved,' I said hastily. 'That shot was perfect.'

'That's because I've gotten to like the game.' He explained that it was because the young ladies played it and said that my stepmother was even going to teach him to play poker. 'I never was much of a man's man, Quint. I never was.' I watched him in silence; I had heard him say this before. 'That's one reason your own mother's death was so hard on me.' I had also heard him say this a good many times before. 'Everyone thought I acted mighty bad when she died. I went off by myself and didn't look at you till you were three weeks old. It was harder on me than it would have been on another man. Why, when I was a traveling man I used to watch the others playing poker on trains and in hotels and warehouses; it used to just get me!' He stood still a moment watching the white cue ball, then turned directly to me. 'It always made me feel such a nobody, and I never would do it.' I observed him with attention as he leaned out over the green baize of the table; and the bright light shone on his head of still thick and still ungraying black hair. I had already had occasion to notice that the wonderfully thick brown hair of my stepmother did not appear so thick or so dark in the strong light at her dressing table, and at this moment I realized that my stepmother must be five, perhaps ten, years older than my father. I was too young myself to say how much older she was. Perhaps she was as much older than Father as she was richer.

Father pocketed the seven ball. He withdrew from the table to rack his own cue and the cues that the girls had left leaning against the couch. He pulled on his coat again, and as he stood working his white shirt cuffs down below his coat sleeves, I noticed his erect figure and handsome face. At that moment he seemed even taller than his usual six feet, and his flannel suit exaggerated his youthful appearance. His expression was serious, and about the extreme regularity of his features there was always an air of innocence and too austere integrity. While he stood thus, he inspired me not with filial respect but with the sort of fleeting admiration I sometimes felt for movie stars. My own father was a picture of youthful virtue justly rewarded. The half-forgotten times when I had seen him in boarding house parlors, in small hotel rooms, on day coaches, returned to me for a minute now and made me aware of the complete elegance of this room. Then the thought that this wasn't anything but a poolroom, no matter how elaborately fitted out with red draperies and green plush couches, strengthened my first impression. And suddenly Father was saying, 'You like it here, don't you, son?'

'Yes, sir,' I said, 'Yes, sir.'

I felt that I liked it here more than he could possibly imagine. To me 'liking it here' meant first of all liking my stepmother, but it included liking everything that belonged to her. Her house was a three-storied mansion in a gated-off city block known as Portland Place, but what recommended it most to me was its being *her* house and, more especially, its actually having been built for her. She would tell me sometimes how the house had been built and named for her the year after she toured Italy with her own papa. 'It was finished the summer before I made my debut,' she said, and she would laugh as she told me how her papa supervised a lot of the work himself. 'He had a funny old linen hat he wore on the back of his head that summer, and I used to tell him he looked like the English archaeologists we saw in Egypt. That pleased him; nearly everything *I* said pleased him. Especially so after Mama died! . . . Mama had died, you see, before Papa and I went to Italy.' Whenever my stepmother digressed this way from a story she was telling me, she usually smiled or even winked at me, as though to apologize—no matter how serious what she was saying was. But this time she didn't smile; her expression grew more serious. 'Papa really built the house for me so that I wouldn't have to go back to the old house in Venderventer Place where I had seen

Mama suffering so long; she died of cancer, and her suffering was horrible, Quint. That was really why we went abroad, to get away for a while.' Then she was smiling again. 'Papa fell in love with Italy on that trip. He was carried away by the idea of building me an Italian palace out here in St. Louis, Missouri, and he spent a big part of the year collecting things to put in this house. He didn't live but a year, himself, after the house was finished; I always suspected that it was the excitement of watching it go up and the constant exasperation with the workmen that affected his heart. Oh, how terribly out of patience he used to get with the workmen! Particularly when they were putting up the tapestries and other things he had brought back from Italy.'

Her papa had named the house *Casa Anna,* and all her friends had teased her about having her name cut in the glass over the front door. She said she thought it was pretty silly herself, though perhaps not half so silly as the cherubs painted on the sky blue ceiling of the drawing room. I always listened very carefully to anything she said about the house. In every room there were gas lighting fixtures as well as electric ones, and she told me that only on one occasion had the whole house been lit by gas. That was on the night of her debut ball. The gas lights had been burned that night as a concession to her papa, who liked the soft light and the shadows and who said you could not have a *really* formal party under the glare of electricity. After the party, when everyone had gone, she and her papa had strolled from room to room watching the servants turn down the lights, both of them dreading to go to their rooms and face the reality that her presentation party in the new house was now a thing of the past. And my stepmother, when she told me about all of this, remarked that that was the last time the gas lights were used except when there was a storm and the electricity was off for a while. Often when I came in from school the afternoon sun would be shining through the cut-glass transom above the doorway; and seeing the words *Casa Anna* thrown on the raisin-colored carpet in the hall, I would think about the things she had told me. Then when I raised my eyes from the carpet to the big Gothic furnishings of the hall and to the stained-glass window above the oak staircase, that dark, gloomy hall gave me the impression of being the brightest and most cheerful of rooms. I would go to the foot of the stairs, and as I pulled off my leather jacket I would call to my stepmother or whistle a tune that she would recognize.

It was because I felt we were so very well off and so happy that I would worry sometimes about accidents. And at other times I would think how foolish it was to worry about accidents, and I would walk through the rooms of the house or along the street saying how happy I was. I would hunt up my father in the library or in the upstairs sitting room in order to put my arms around his neck in a silent expression of gratitude. 'You like it here, son?' Father would say then, and I could not make an answer. I began to think that my father's wisdom and strength and good faith were almost superhuman, for our present household represented the faithful keeping of promises that he might very well not have been able to keep. Remembering those promises sometimes set me to thinking about the days when he had made them. I could remember his saying things to me about *amounting to something* when I was no more than five or six years old, when I was still staying with my grandmother in Tennessee. But I remembered more distinctly things he said the year we were living in Louisville. We lived in a good boarding house there, better than any place we had lived in before, and we each had a big room with a double bed. We had a private bathroom with a tile shower, and we had a little porch of our own. A Negro maid served us breakfast in our rooms; we ate dinner in the big restaurants and cafeterias downtown. Twice that winter Father took me to St. Louis, where I met the president and several vice-presidents of the hardware company, and I remember the president's taking me aside to tell me that that father of mine had a real head on his shoulders, a real drive about him and good business sense. On the first trip we stayed at the Chase Hotel. I spent most of the days in our room, gazing out the window or sailing paper arrows out over Lindell Boulevard toward Forest Park. Once I looked down into the street to see my father getting out of a taxi with two other men, and it was strange to realize that I could not have distinguished him from the other men on the sidewalk except for the old-fashioned broad-brimmed hat he wore. On the second trip we stayed at the president's house and came back to Louisville on a Pullman. 'If ever I get to be anybody,' Father promised me then, 'we'll live in St. Louis all the time.'

That winter in Louisville Father took me to several picture shows. Neither of us had seen many motion pictures before this, and when we came back to the boarding house after a show, Father seemed always excited and full of talk. If the movie was about poor people he would talk of the days when he had first left the farm. If it was about rich people he would talk of the friends he had made in St. Louis and say that in a few years he and I would *have things* and *be somebody* ourselves. Once on a rainy night we came in from seeing a picture that was all about Abe Lincoln, and when we opened the front door, we could hear the telephone ringing. It would give a long ring and then there would be a little nervous tinkling. Father said, 'That's long-distance,' and he hurried to answer it. The call was for him. He stood talking for ten minutes to the Chattanooga office. Finally he put down the receiver, and bending over the telephone table, he made some notations on a pad there. Then he looked up at me, and I could see that he was going to talk, could tell it by the faraway, squinted-up look in his eye and by the way he pushed his new Homburg on the back of his head and began to loosen his silk necktie. 'One time, son,' he commenced abruptly, 'I tried to get a job with a furniture concern in Chattanooga. I was stopping in Franklin at the time, trying to marry your mother, and so I tried to clinch the job by long-distance from my hotel room in Franklin. I talked to Chattanooga five times in one day. The sales manager encouraged me and said he would write me.' Now and then Father would look down at the telephone as he talked. 'But after a week I still hadn't heard from him. So I went to a friend of mine who had recommended me for the job and asked him to send a telegram to Chattanooga.'

'Did they have telegrams then?' I asked.

'So this friend of mine,' he continued, as though I hadn't said anything, 'showed me a letter the sales manager had written him. It said my experience was inadequate for dealing with high-powered customers that I'd have to contact in Grand Rapids and New York. The sales manager never wrote me a line, and my telephone bill was thirteen dollars.'

'Did you have the money to pay for the calls?' I asked.

'Yes, but your mother and I only went to Bershebe Springs on our honeymoon. We wanted to go to Washington, D.C.'

'Did you ever see the sales manager since, Father?'

'Many times.' He shook his head with a little laugh. 'He's a peach of a fellow. He just didn't know how to tell me no. But every time I hear an operator saying, 'Chattanooga calling,' even nowadays, I have a sudden queer feeling of hope and then of disappointment.

That fellow was dead right, though, about my experience. I had only worked country towns with hardware then.'

The next year, when I was ten, we moved to St. Louis. We arrived there on a morning in the first part of September, and on the very day of our arrival my father took me to enroll in the public school on Union Street. It was the biggest school I had ever seen. As we went up the steps Father held my hand and said, 'It's big, but you'll get used to it.' I looked up at the three-story building and thought that I had never seen so many windows or so many green window shades. Inside, the wide hall was lined with green metal lockers, and there were hundreds of children rushing about and paying no attention to one another. My father continued to reassure me: 'You'll get used to it. It won't seem so big after a few days.' But Father himself was turning first one way and then another, until at last I stepped up to a table where an old man sat reading the morning paper.

'Where do you register for the fifth?' I asked.

The old man, whom I now recognized by his clothes as the janitor, gave me directions, and I led my father up the stairs to the second floor. 'I want to meet your teacher,' Father said. 'In a place this big I ought at least to know your teacher.' When we were in the classroom the teacher, whose name was Miss Moore, shook my father's hand, as a man would do, and she told him about the school and then a lot of things about St. Louis. Presently she shook my hand, told me that I had a splendid name, and pointed out a seat to me at the back of the room. From there I watched them talking, and I could see that Father was still saying how big the school was and how big St. Louis was. I began to look about me. I was in a room full of boys and girls, a long, high-ceilinged room with a row of tall windows on one side and blackboards on the other. I was in the fifth grade and this would be the seventh school I had attended. This one, I thought, I should like best of all, because this one was the biggest of all and nobody would know that I was a new boy.

It turned out that Miss Moore was not my teacher after all; I was moved the following day into another section. Yet whenever I passed her in the halls she remembered me and smiled. One morning she stopped me and gave me an envelope to take to my father. I watched her that day with the other teachers in the lunchroom; I decided that perhaps she was pretty. Although her mouth seemed too crowded with teeth and her hair was cut like a man's, she had such a pleasant way with her that it was hard to say she wasn't pretty. That night I delivered the envelope to my father, who at once opened it and read aloud to me her invitation to a church supper after which there would be a musical program. She wrote that she had thought of my father because he had seemed genuinely interested when she talked about the music classes at the school and about the summer operas in the park. Father handed me the note and said, 'I think we might go. It might be a good idea.' And we did go, but afterward I could never forget the shocked expression on Miss Moore's face when I followed Father into the Sunday School room where the long supper tables were set. She stood a moment looking at me as though she didn't know who I was or as though she had suddenly thought of something she had left on the stove. But the next time she invited Father somewhere, she made a point of planning entertainment that both of us could enjoy. Whenever they went anywhere together I was taken along. Sometimes we would all go riding in her blue sedan on Sunday afternoons. We would drive across the river into Illinois or on a pretty day we would drive out the St. Charles Rock Road to a little town where, she told us, the old inhabitants still spoke only French. Father would turn to me and say, 'Now isn't that interesting, Quint?'

One night Miss Moore came in her sedan to take us to a concert at the Mozart Club. I saw her leaning across the front seat and watching us as we came down the steps to the sidewalk. I noticed that she didn't greet us as cordially as usual, and then when Father had opened the car door and put one foot on the running board, I heard her say to him, 'Why, Gerald, I believe you forgot to change from your business shoes.'

Father was dressed in a new tuxedo. He looked down at the brown shoe on the running board, and blushing deeply along the flat planes of his cheeks, he said, 'What . . . what . . . yes, I have. Why, I have, Miss

Moore.' (He usually called her by her Christian name, but he had this time said 'Miss Moore' as though she were his teacher too.) Stepping backward and out onto the sidewalk he said, 'You'll have to wait on me. Come on, Quint. Come with me, quick now.'

As we went into the vestibule of our boarding house he told me to go to every door on the first floor until I found a roomer who would lend him a pair of black shoes. And he hurried up to the second and third floors to canvass the rooms there. After a while I came up to his room with a pair of heavy black leather oxfords which I had borrowed from the German janitor. I found Father standing at the front window of his room, looking down at Miss Moore's automobile. Without turning around he said, 'No luck, I suppose?'

'Yess'r,' I said. I walked across the room and put the shoes on the sill before him.

'Whose are they?' he asked, hardly glancing at them.

'The janitor's.' Then I too looked down into the street and saw the sedan with the door still standing open the way Father had left it.

Finally he picked up the shoes and began loosening the laces. When he had put them on he said, 'The right one's a little small.' I looked up at him and felt that I had never seen him appear so uncomfortable and so angular, so much like the uncles at my grandma's when they were leaving for church. We started to leave, but at the door he suddenly stopped me. 'This won't happen again, Quint,' he said. 'I can promise you that. But you remember it. Don't *ever* forget tonight, son. You and I must learn these things.' I did remember it, and nothing at the concert that night impressed me so much as the high polish on the violinist's patent-leather shoes. Afterward I remembered that night as the last time we ever went anywhere with Miss Moore, and I supposed it was partly because that was not long before Father met Mrs. Lauterbach and began taking her to dinner parties at Mr. Colby's house and to dances at the country club.

Soon after Christmas that year he told me that he had been made a vice-president of the company. His picture was in the paper, and he showed me letters he had received inviting him to join a country club and a men's town club on Kings Highway. 'All that can wait till you're a little older,' he said. We still lived in a boarding house where most of the other roomers were drummers and railroad men, but he said there was no use in moving until we got a permanent place. And he said I was safer there under the eyes of the German landlady than I would be in an apartment of our own. Since at that time he was beginning to go out in the evening a good deal, he was probably thinking more of my loneliness than of my safety. As he left the house he would usually tell me to go down to the boarders' parlor and talk to the men or send me into old Mrs. Frenz's sitting room. One night when he was going out for dinner, Mrs. Frenz said to me in his presence, 'Your fod-ther is popular and vell-liked.' Father was by the front door pulling on his gloves. He looked at the landlady and said in his usual literal way:

'No, Mrs. Frenz. It's only they always like a single man at these parties. Even the middle-aged people here like to have single men for the single women at their parties.'

Mrs. Frenz answered genially, 'Yes, and soon you are not a single man any more, maybe?'

Father smiled broadly. 'There,' said the landlady, 'I have made your fod-ther smile. I think I have hit the truth.'

Sometimes Father and I went to movies together at night, and some nights I went with him to his office and got up my lessons there or merely looked at the pictures on the walls of the conference room, which was across the hall from his office. I was in that conference room one night, sitting at the end of the long green table and gazing up at a picture of the founder of the company, when I realized that Father had entered the room and was taking a seat at the other end of the table. I smiled at him, but he seemed completely unaware of anything funny about our sitting like this in the conference room at past nine o'clock in the evening.

'Are you ready to go?' I asked, closing the book which was still open to the first page of my lesson.

He didn't answer. He turned in the straight armchair, looked up at the pictures on the paneled walls, and crossed his legs in a tense and thoughtful way. I could see his right knee sticking up above the table. After a moment he began abruptly, 'I had a dream last night. I dreamed that . . . that you, that I, rather, had gotten married to a woman—the very nicest sort of woman —and that you liked her just as much as I did and were very glad I was married and that we were living in a house I had bought and were about as happy as we could be—with somebody to look after us, you know. . . . Quint, it seemed like this woman was kind of young—much younger than your grandma, for instance, and was a person more like yourself and who had always lived here in St. Louis . . . and known people.'

Not for a moment did I believe that Father had had such a dream, but at the time I didn't try to explain his pretending he had. Instead, I tried to conceal my disbelief and embarrassment by beginning at once to tell a dream I had had last night. When I had finished telling my own dream I felt that it had been the wrong thing to do, but I couldn't quite be sorry that I had done it. I looked from my father to the picture of the company's founder and to the pictures of the various officers and directors that were on the wall. And I looked at the group pictures of them, which had been taken in this very room. Glancing at Father again, I saw him seated still at the other end of the table with his eyes fixed meaningfully on me, his expression so like that on all the faces pictured on the wall that it made goose bumps rise on my arms. And then it seemed perfectly explicit to me why he had not thought it funny for us to sit together at this table while he talked that nonsense about that dream he had not had. I realized at that moment that I had always hated what they called my father's 'business drive,' and simultaneously I realized that I was myself the very center and core of it, that the decisions Father sometimes had to make at this table were, for all practical purposes, decisions about me.

Father said no more that night. In a few minutes we put out the lights and went home to our boarding house on Washington Boulevard.

My stepmother was fond of saying that most young people were mere caricatures of their elders. 'Quint,' she liked to say, 'is the only child I know that has any dignity of his own.' She said that it was a quality I had brought with me from the farm in Tennessee where I was born. Then she would wink at me or give me a big hug and say, 'I guess you have a sort of animal dignity, like your papa.' That was her way of poking her gentle fun at me, for she seemed bound to poke her gentle fun at everybody. She said that her husband had an animal dignity but that also he had another dignity to distinguish him from the men she knew here in St. Louis. She said it was always just when she had decided Father was hard as nails and the typical self-made man of business that she discovered something courtly, or at least something hopelessly old-fashioned, in him. She pretended to complain that he baffled her German servants, treating them sometimes as equals and sometimes as black body servants who might at any time be sent to the fields if they didn't toe the line. Whenever Father said something that puzzled her she would say, 'I can't decide whether you're a Kentucky colonel or a Mr. Go-getter.' Her daughters' slang and their views on who and what was important in their lives were often the objects of her fun poking. She would wickedly lead Bess into defining the Social Position of some neighbor in Portland Place; she would pretend to agree with her, saying between bursts of laughter, 'They're really nobody, aren't they, Bess? They're really nobody!' Or she would encourage Laura, who had a moderate flair for mimicry, in ridiculing some family friend or relative; but when Laura had finished, she was likely to hear herself being mimicked by her own mother. Mother could remember just the thing Laura had said to that very relative on his last visit: 'Uncle Frederick, I think that Paisley tie you're wearing is a perfect knockout.' Only once, however, did I ever see a sign of ill humor in my stepmother's teasing, and that was a time when Laura had mimicked my own accent and laughed at my long Latin name. Then Mother had simply lowered her eyes and mockingly repeated her daughter's surname: 'Lauterrrbach.'

On my twelfth birthday my stepmother gave me a party. It was held in the basement game room. After the party, when I was looking over the presents again, I took up the watch my own Grandma Lovell had sent from Tennessee. It had come through the mail several days before, heavily insured and wrapped in a box five times the size of the plain black case. My stepmother would not allow me to open the package until the morning of my birthday, and I had not insisted. I was a little afraid of what Grandma might have seen fit to send a twelve-year-old boy. It was never anything new she sent me, something out of the house, a keepsake of my dead mother or of my grandfather, an old book, something queer or country that the boys in St. Louis would laugh at. I took the package up to my room to open it.

It contained a big gold watch with a lid that snapped to over the face and a dial marked with Roman numerals. I recalled my grandmother's having shown me this watch during summers that I had spent with her, and she had promised that it should be mine on my twenty-first birthday. But she had sent it on my twelfth, instead. My surprise and delight could not have been greater. I hurried down the back stairway (the route I always took when in haste) and through the kitchen and pantry to the dining room where the family were still at breakfast with the morning papers all over the table. I exhibited the watch first to my father and then to my stepmother and sisters. The girls especially admired the elaborate initials of my grandfather engraved on the lid: Q.C.L. My stepmother remarked that it was actually quite a handsome heirloom. And Father began to talk of what a fine old gentleman Grandpa Lovell had been, and he said that my mother's people had been people of considerable means in the old days and that Grandma Lovell was an aristocrat of the old Southern school.

'I should like to meet her some day, Gerald,' my

stepmother said to him. 'She must be fine.' Then turning to me she said, 'Come let your mother bestow a birthday kiss, young man.' I went forward to receive the kiss. I liked to be fondled by my stepmother. (I thought sometimes that it was on account of me that Father had married her.) At the very first I had thought that maybe it was only the pleasant roundness of her arms and the soft wave in her hair that attracted me to her. But soon I knew that it was more even than the feel of her cheek on my forehead when she would hug me to herself saying, 'I always wanted a boy, and now I have one of my very own.' From the outset I sensed that she wanted me as I wanted her. The real strength and comfort I derived from her came afterward, but even before the wedding took place I had begun to call her 'Mother.'

Father was talking at length to the girls about Grandma and the Lovell home place, Belgrove. I could not deny the truth of what he was saying, but I suspected that it was the sight of the gold watch that made him describe them so glowingly. My father never lied, I had heard Grandma say, but he never told but one set of truths at a time. Sometimes I had heard him describe Grandma as a poor-little-old country woman with a run-down farm. This morning he talked of her bed with the half canopy and of the cannon on the lawn and the stack of rusty shells on the ell porch. I could think only of the privy down by the chicken yard at Belgrove and the sound of Grandma's guinea-like voice waking the whole house at six A.M. Finally Mother interrupted Father with her usual banter: 'Ah, me, Colonel Dudley. When you talk that way, my heart beats faster and I'm sure there's Southern blood in my veins.' He grinned indulgently and commenced eating his breakfast again.

I carried the watch about in my shirt pocket all day, occasionally feeling with my hand to make sure it was safe. The first guests arrived at the party and delivered their presents ceremoniously but saying only, 'Here.' I arranged the gifts on a table that was cleared for them. I did not wait long to place the watch among the other presents (without the old-fashioned case in which it had arrived). The bicycle and the electric jigsaw that Father and Mother had given me were on exhibit in my workshop adjoining the game room. But it was the watch which I expected to excite most comment.

I wasn't mistaken. Dick Morrison said, 'That's the niftiest alarm clock I've ever seen. You could almost carry it in your pocket.' Dick's sayings were famous and this one was too wonderful to miss. The little girls giggled and the boys howled and slapped themselves on the head and pretended to swallow their fists. At a twelve-year-old party in St. Louis it was permissible that some gifts be mere jokes, and so there was a good proportion of rattles and baby toys and even a razor. But nothing caused so much mirth as the watch. When the hall clock chimed upstairs, a little girl asked if that were my watch. I tried to join in the fun, and putting the watch in my pocket, I pretended that my knees buckled under its weight.

But when all the guests had been called for by parents and chauffeurs and maids, I took the watch upstairs and put it away in the drawer with my Bible and ear muffs and white silk scarf. It was only a piece of junk now. I could still hear their laughter after I got in bed that night, and though I kept telling myself that I had got off some of the very best cracks about the watch myself, I said, 'Why am I so dumb, God? Why didn't I see it was only an old piece of junk from the start? Why didn't I see Laura and Bess were only being polite about it because this was my birthday?' The next morning I awoke, as I often did, with a renewed sense of my own ignorance and a fresh desire to break open the little locks on my stepsisters' diaries. I sat up on the side of the bed, determined to think no more about the silly old watch; then involuntarily I sank back on the bed and lay there for a long time, thinking not about the watch but about my grandmother's farm and the long visits I used to make there. My very earliest recollection was of the last day of one of those visits to Belgrove. I remember going into the side yard where the other children—my cousins—were looking for something in the grass. I heard them speaking of it as though it were a familiar thing, each saying where he had seen it last. I followed after them, looking harder than any of the rest. Finally they found it. It was very useful looking, and it was right where Reba had put it by the trellis. They held it too high for me to see what it was. But finally they had found it, and I shouted for joy with the rest of them. Suddenly I reached for it with both hands, and Reba and Jeff and Rob at once began slapping at my hands as was customary and saying, 'No, Quint, . . . your daddy wouldn't want you to. He wouldn't have you touch it.' They held it higher and higher. 'No, Quint. No.'

At almost the same instant Grandma and old Aunt Muncie began calling from the busted-out wicker chairs:

'Keep it away from that baby!'

'You'll all be punished if he gets a spot on him!'

And then all the children, including those who were not a bit of kin, began to speak almost in a chorus, 'No, Quint, no!' They lifted the thing higher and higher, and the sun shone on its red rusty surface.

Later they left it by the porch steps, and I found it there. I picked it up, calling it by the name I pretended always to have known, and I made a noise like the one Jeff had made, pretending that I knew what it was used for. Then I put it down and went and searched in the high grass by the fence where I had not thought to look before. But this time I knew what I was looking for and really I knew where it was, which made the search somewhat different. Pretending that I was one of the strange children from down at the Fork, I asked myself what I was looking for. Then I said what it was, shrugging my shoulders indifferently. I walked along the garden fence with my hands on my hips, pretending to whistle, which I had not yet learned to do, and telling myself that I knew my way around the farm as well as the cousins who lived there all the time. But when I reached the corner of the pasture I felt uncomfortable and a little lost. I was glad when they called to me from the porch, and when I turned around I was glad to see the bright yellow taxicab, with the black lattice painted on its doors, bumping along the gravel lane between the dark cedar trees. It was my father. My summer visit to Grandma's was over. My father would kiss Grandma if she let him, and then as he put me in the taxicab, Grandma would begin talking fast, talking more than she had all summer, saying what a shame it was about me, and what was to become of me? In the taxicab we would ride along the pike, past the old toll gate, over the long plank bridge, and into Franklin. From Franklin we would ride on the electric inter-urban to Nashville. And from Nashville we would ride on a real train to wherever we were going to live that winter.

On my grandmother's farm there was only one white oak tree left; it grew in the field between the greenhouse and the old tobacco barn. Every summer when I was visiting, Grandma used to take the other children and me down in the field and point out the white oak to us. We always went by way of the Indian graveyard which made the whole west side of her shady lawn uneven, but she never allowed the children to walk on the graves. She would lead us, stepping carefully between the graves; and all the children following after her would reverently put their feet down like hers between the grass-covered mounds. Yet when Grandma had gone back to the house, I would watch Rob and Jeff running helter-skelter over the graves and even digging into them for arrowheads and skinning knives. It was only upon the graves of the two Indian children that they would not walk or play. For Grandma said the graves contained children of peaceful Indians who fell victim to the more barbarous nations. Once when I stepped on one of those graves by mistake, Rob threatened to lock me away in the cellar. And Jeff agreed that that was their rule.

They had a rule too about playing in the old abandoned schoolhouse. There you were never allowed to speak above a whisper, for the schoolhouse had been shelled during the Battle of Nashville and there was a story that some of the Confederate children had been killed. Yet in the old trenches, where the soldiers had bled and grass grew like a carpet, the boys shouted and fought or sometimes lay still and played that they were the dead Confederate soldiers.

There was only the one white oak, and there was only one magnolia tree left on Grandma's farm. The magnolia grew in the side yard by the ell porch, and they used to tell me how my mother, who died when I was born, used to play in it when she was a little girl. It seemed that the magnolia was always in bloom when Father and I first came in the summertime, and Father would say that it reminded him of a tree on the farm where he was raised. Sometimes as we came through the yard he would say, 'Take off your shoes, son, and go barefooted in the grass. I want to see you do it and remember how it feels.' But Grandma, sitting on the porch, would scoff at him and twist about in her chair. She would look down from the porch at Father as though to discover anew what sort of man this son-in-law of hers was. For she knew, as I did, that after a few minutes Father was certain to say to me, 'Put on your shoes again, Quint. There are too many rusty nails on a farm.' And when the week end was over and Father was leaving—he never stayed but the week end—he would call her aside and say, 'I prefer that Quint play close about the premises of the house, Mother Lovell. . . . He's mostly a city boy, not on to country things like the others.' Grandma would nod, but when he was gone she would send me off, sometimes against my own wishes, with my cousins and the little Negroes on their expeditions to Radnor Lake or Wild Man's Hill.

I remember one morning when I came down to breakfast and found Father—his straw hat on his head and his brief case in hand—standing in the pantry doorway. His back was to the dining room, and I could not see my grandmother whom he was addressing in the pantry: 'I have told you so darned many times, Mother Lovell.'

Grandma's voice came more distinctly than his. 'I must say it's very difficult for me to comply, though I do try. Indeed, I do.'

From the dining room I could see Father shaking his head nervously and beating his brief case against his right knee. He managed to say only again and again, 'But I have told you so many times, Mother Lovell.'

Presently the old woman appeared to my sight beyond Father in the pantry. She had come and was
standing before him, looking directly into the face that
I could not see. 'You must try to trust me. I have tried
to use my own judgment, but I won't do that again.
You must try to trust me again, Gerald, to do just as
you say.' I could tell that Father had threatened not to
let me come back another summer.

'But I've told you—'

'I don't always really understand you, son,' she said
vaguely. 'I've raised my own children differently—the
way your own mother must have done hers, Gerald. It
seems second nature. And children *learn* things on a
farm, real things—even about the animals.'

'What I want seems darned simple to me,' Father
said in exhaustion. 'Must I put down boundaries and
stipulate as though—'

'As though I were a hired Negro girl off Beale Street.'
Her lips were suddenly drawn tight over her false
teeth. Father turned and looked at me over his shoulder, and I felt guilty for having answered any of Grandma's questions about Father and me. 'Leave the boy
with me,' she said while Father's back was turned to
her. 'Give him to me, Gerald. It's better to grow up in
the country. It's what people need.'

'No, Mother Lovell!' His back was to me again. 'Not
any more, it isn't, and hasn't been for a long time.
Quint needs other things.'

'He needs a mother!'

'He needs a mother who has never seen a farm. He

needs to go to city schools where they teach you something, and he needs money.'

As Father spoke he was backing through the doorway toward me, and Grandma's expression changed again. 'I'll try to do as you say in these matters,' she said. Father stooped down and put his arm about my shoulders. Then he went up through the house to the front porch to see if the taxicab had come from Franklin. When he had driven away in the taxi, Grandma called me into the pantry and held my hand while she gave out the lunches she had packed for the cousins and for the two Negro children. They were leaving for a swimming expedition to Brown's Creek. One lunch, wrapped in brown oiled paper, was left on the pantry cupboard.

The other children went outside, and you could still hear the sound of ponies in the lane when she began to explain to me why I could not go along. But I drew away from her as she spoke. She had already begun her morning dusting, and she followed me out onto the porch with a great turkey feather duster in her hand. All at once I leapt off the porch and ran down the lawn away from her. I knew that if I stayed, she would soon be asking me how many schools my father had put me in last year and wanting to know if I were going to grow up to sell hardware and be forever moving around from pillar to post. I ran down the lawn toward the little brick dependency that was known as the Office. As I ran over the flat lawn, I had a glimpse of an ancient hitching ring in the side of a giant oak. It had been almost entirely swallowed up in the growth of the old tree, and that section of the ring which was visible stuck in my mind. I went into the single, empty room of the Office and shut the door. The room was unfurnished but for a battered old roll-top desk by the far wall. The iron grate was lying on the hearth before the fireplace, and in the center of the floor was a heap of dried dog excrement. I sat down on the wide sill of one of the windows and tried to imagine the appearance of this room when my grandfather had been alive and engaged in some business here. But for me that was as unreal as the thought that the iron hitching ring had once hung usefully from a slender oak. I turned and looked out the window and saw my grandmother still standing on the porch with her feather duster. I knew that she was watching me and waiting for me to come back to the house. For a moment I longed to go and throw my arms about her waist and perhaps to cry in her apron, but presently I knew I could not and that I never would be able to.

The next winter when I was staying with Father in the boarding house at Louisville, I would think how glad I was that he didn't ask me about my life with Grandma in the summertime. He seemed to know all about it. Whenever I did talk about things that happened at the farm, he would listen patiently but without interest; and when I had finished he would say, 'Yes. . . . Yes, but you're mostly a town boy, aren't you? You're mostly a city boy.' Once he said to me, 'You lack that faculty to learn things that must be learned on a farm. You don't *really* like to work with your hands or to be outdoors.' He told me about the things he had learned when he was a farm boy himself and how it never helped him any to know those things when he went into business. 'We had only a poor ridge farm,' he said, 'and we fought nature with nature. We always let the martins bin up in the eaves of our house to drive off the hawks. How they did used to scare me when they whizzed past my window upstairs at night. Our house was a real old timer with the eaves coming right down over the little square upstairs windows. There were no windows at all in the gables.' He talked without sentiment, as though he were merely giving evidence. 'There were always snakes in the corn crib to keep the rats away. And my daddy would never let us kill a skunk—not even the nasty one that had her kittens under our house one year—because he said they killed rats and kept away varmints. You learn a lot of things in the country, especially where there are no niggers around to get between you and the real work, but a mighty lot of good it did me when I went into hardware.'

There was one quarrel that I had with my father during the first winter in my stepmother's house. Then I had it again at Christmas time. By Easter it didn't matter so much, and in June I conceded privately that I had been, myself, unreasonable. It was about school. They had entered me in the Country Day School for

Boys, and I had wanted to continue at the ugly old public school where I had been the year before.

'I don't want to go to school all day,' I had argued.

'Why, son, it's not all school. You have athletics in the afternoon.'

'I don't want games every afternoon.'

'It's not games every day, Quint. Some days you follow your special hobby.'

'I don't have any hobby. And I don't like being out in the country.'

'It's not really the country. It's the suburbs.'

Then I would go to my room on the verge of tears; for my father had answered all my arguments and yet I had not even presented my honest objection. I considered this objection of such a private nature that it could not be mentioned. It reflected my own weakness too clearly and could not fail to call that weakness to my father's attention. It would reveal to the whole family how little self-confidence I had among people of my own age.

Its concealment was dear to me. Only so long as my family was kept in ignorance did I believe I could endure my own growing consciousness of it. For the five years before my father had met and married Mrs. Lauterbach I had been going to school. And during those years I had been enrolled in seven different schools. Now this would be my eighth. It was the thought of taking my obscure place among a crowd of strangers in such a small private school that made me argue with Father. I knew how the first day would be and I knew how things would be afterward. I knew that the year would end with me still a stranger, watching enviously those self-assured, popular boys who dominated everything.

Yet I went to the new school. For me it was the same old six-and-seven. I didn't get laughed at or get my feelings hurt, and nobody acted snotty or tried to pick a fight with me, all because I didn't even try to make friends right at first. I didn't study (because nobody can study at a new school) and I didn't pretend to study. I just made passing grades and went my own way as though I didn't care about anything or anybody in the school. I might as well; I had learned that. It was hard and I hated myself for turning up my nose at those who did try to be friendly with me, but they were always the untouchables and the awful-phonies. If you had any get-up-and-go about you, you couldn't afford to make friends with them.

The first school year was uneventful until the last day. During the winter Mother had given me that birthday party. She had invited children of her friends, and although most of the boys turned out to be from my own school and class, I did not try to be friendly with them afterward. I simply went to their parties in return and that was the end of it. I might not have been able to hold out so independently had there been less that was new and exciting to occupy me at home. When I came home in the afternoons and found Laura and Bess with some of their friends in the drawing room, and Mother and Father waiting for me in the library, I completely forgot everything that had happened during the day. But during the morning recess on the very last day of school I provoked a fight with Dick Morrison. I was not sure myself whether or not I did it on purpose, but I knew that after such a fight everybody would at least remember me if I came back a second year.

When I started for home that afternoon after the fight there was a bluish splotch on my left temple. Because it was the last day of school, the streetcar we called the Special left the school siding an hour early, at four o'clock. I climbed aboard and saw one of the boys pointing out my bruise to a group that was gathered around the conductor. Then I knew they were telling the conductor about the fight. When the streetcar finally moved off, I was sitting by a window. The sunlight was just different enough from the light at the usual hour of this ride to hold my attention. But after the first impression of strangeness, I watched the passing fields and scattered buildings with a greater sense of my own familiarity with the route through the suburbs. The two boys in the seat in front of me began to talk about good-old Country Day and the good-old Special and to say they guessed there was nothing else quite like this good-old ride on the Special every day. But I was recalling scenes that had become familiar to me while going to and from other schools. I sat by the window continually searching with my forefinger for the sorest spot in my bruise and wondering if I would be returning to Country Day next year.

My stepmother's black limousine was pulling into the porte-cochere as I cut across the lawn that afternoon. It was late but it was still quite sunny. I was carrying all of the books and tablets that had collected in my desk through the year; because my cap was set on the side of my head, the bill did not protect my eyes from the sun. The sunlight struck my eyes so directly that I could hardly recognize my stepmother as she came across the grass to meet me. She was hurrying toward me to take some of my books, and I realized that as she came she was trying to determine what the dark place on my temple was.

'Why, Quint!' she called out; she began to run. Before I knew it she had reached me and was taking my books and kneeling before me on the grass. I could not attend to what she was saying, nor answer her questions, nor respond to her sympathy; for my whole attention was caught at first by the careless motion with which she fell to her knees—careless of her clothing and her comfort and her dignity—and now I became engrossed in the detail of the alligator purse that she had flung to the ground and which now lay open with half its red and black accessories spilled out in the fresh green grass.

At last I looked up at her and said hoarsely, 'I had a fight.'

'Quint Dudley!' She was examining the bruise. She

asked me what it was I had fought about.

'I don't know.'

She smiled. 'Just say you don't want to tell an old woman.'

'Oh, I don't know, I don't!'

My stepmother's smile faded as she pretended to interest herself in the bruise.

'Mother, tell me,' I demanded in an urgent whisper, 'am I going back next year . . . to Country Day?'

'Of course you are if you want to.'

'If I don't go back, I don't want to go to school anywhere, not to any more schools.'

Then Mother looked into my face, for several minutes it seemed. Finally she stood up with all the books in her arms and motioned for me to gather her purse and its spilled contents. I followed her into the house and up the carpeted stairs to my own room on the third floor. She dumped the books on the bed as roughly as I might have done. 'Let's have a game of rummy,' she said. And she pulled off her hat in the reckless way that Laura and Bess pulled off their hats sometimes. There was a little warm breeze blowing outside, and when I opened a window the curtains kept blowing in across the bed. 'Tie 'em together, old boy,' she said. But I pushed the curtains back and fastened them neatly, as I knew she would want me to do. The game proceeded, and we played until we heard the sound of Father's automobile in the driveway below. Then my stepmother went over and, raising the screen, she leaned far out the window. I came and leaned out beside her; and she called to my father on the pavement three floors below, 'Come on up! School's out and we're having a grand time!' Father laughed and waved his evening paper at us.

Mother looked at herself in the mirror over my dresser. 'I must go down and fix myself,' she said. But before she left the room she came and sat down on the bed. As she gathered up the playing cards she said, 'You've come to stay, Quint. There are going to be no more new schools and no more strange children to go among. Unless you want to, you are never going to go to any other school and you are never going to live in any other house than mine.' Wrinkling up her forehead and placing her hand on mine, she continued, 'You must stop supposing that things will change and you must stop being afraid that you and I will not always have each other, Quint. Next year you must go back to school and make your way. Somehow I mean to help you, but all a mother can do is to always believe you're right about everything. And I don't think that'll be hard for me.' It was just as though I had come to her with everything that had ever worried me, and she had known how to comfort me. I wondered how I had ever lived without her. She stood up to go, but instead of leaving, she went and sat on the arm of a little upholstered chair that was slipcovered in chintz. 'I'll bet you don't like this chair in here,' she said rather absent-mindedly.

'I'd rather have a leather one.' I smiled. 'With a footstool.'

'We'll have to look into that.' I could tell by the way she said it that she wasn't really thinking about the chair, and I wondered if she weren't still thinking about my going back to Country Day. 'Quint,' she said after a moment, 'when I was a little older than you are—when I was thirteen—I'd been going to the Institute here in St. Louis for eight years, and I loved it. I loved all my little chums and my music teacher and especially my governess, named Miss McLeod. I loved my papa and mama and our old house in Vanderventer Place, and I loved all the servants and even the carriage horses Charlie and Pat.' Now she moved from the arm into the chair. 'What a thrill it was to look out the window just before school was out and see the carriage and horses waiting beyond the high iron fence. Sometimes I could see the shadowy figure of Miss McLeod waiting for me inside the carriage. How I loved the sight of them there. I can't think of anything I *didn't* love.'

I laughed aloud at this, and Mother laughed too. 'Oh, I loved everything,' she said. Then I realized that I wasn't laughing merely at Mother's saying she loved all those things. I was laughing from pure delight at the thought of her as a little girl riding in a carriage. She didn't say anything for a minute, and through the open window I heard the noise of traffic over on Lindell Boulevard and the rumbling of a streetcar that would have been the Special at this time on ordinary days. Mother wasn't smiling when she began speaking again.

'But when I was thirteen Mama thought I ought to go to a school in Switzerland while she and Papa spent the winter in Karlsruhe for her health. I shuddered at the idea of leaving St. Louis and being separated from Mama and Papa and Miss McLeod. But Mama was in 'declining health'—that's what they always used to say. And I tried to please her in everything, because Papa was so impatient with her. So I did go to Switzerland to school. . . . We sailed from Boston—all six of us, for we took two maids and Miss McLeod along to see after us. Mama took seven trunks, I remember. The maids were forever bragging about that; I once heard old Minnie tell a cleaning woman in a London hotel that Papa was the richest man west of Chicago.'

'*Was* he, Mother?' To me the phrase sounded like something out of a Western story.

'No. Of course he wasn't. But we were very rich, Quint—the way people aren't rich any more, some-how. Yet I had never thought of our being so rich before we left St. Louis and went to Europe. Nobody—nothing—ever made me so conscious of it as the girls at St. Clair's, the school I went to in Switzerland. They were girls who came mostly from fine European families, but their families didn't have money any more; and it seemed that that was all in me that interested them: my money. I soon found out that even those I was most friendly with always spoke of me as 'the millionairess' behind my back. . . . That was what they called me: the American millionairess. And I knew that was what made some of them want to go with me to

Karlsruhe for the holidays. I would have delighted in bringing along a visitor to Karlsruhe, and Papa urged me to. But whenever I was about to invite some girl, she always said something that made me think she didn't like me for myself.'

While Mother talked she had completely forgotten that Father was waiting for her downstairs, and when we heard him calling from the foot of the stairs, she jumped suddenly to her feet. With a look of agitation on her face she said, 'Your father's home!' as though she didn't remember waving to him out the window a few minutes before.

During the summer Father and Mother and I went to Harbor Point, in Michigan, as Mother had always done. The girls, of course, went to join their real father and the Madam at Bar Harbor. All summer long cards and letters kept coming from the girls with postscripts to say hello to some 'cute boy' or to a schoolmate; for at the Point there were exactly those people whom I had been seeing at my stepmother's house through the winter. One of Laura's first letters told about the Madam's absence. Another letter said that she had gone to Reno. Later in the summer they wrote of their father's engagement to a woman they called the New Madam. We were on the screened porch that overlooked the lake when Mother read this letter to Father and me. Father looked at me to see if I were following it; I pretended to be studying the funnies.

'I think we should send for the girls,' Father said.

'It is a pity they can't be with us at the Point,' she answered rather indifferently, 'but their father must see them at every stage of growing up. This was all agreed to.'

'But they've no business being there right *now*.'

'It won't hurt them.'

'It won't help them any.'

'It might. My girls have got to learn faster than others. It makes a difference when children have their own money. Their father long ago made them independent of me.'

'But it's not a matter of money.'

'Well, it's a matter of business—in a larger sense, that is. It's hard to know where one thing ends and another begins, so you might as well take it all as one dose. I do know that if I hadn't been so generally sheltered as a young thing, the storm mightn't have seemed so terrific.'

'Why, I didn't think there *was* much of a storm.'

'There wasn't, Gerald,' she said with an exaggeratedly frank smile. 'I only like to talk that romantic way about the divorce sometimes. It's the last remnant of girlishness in me. Actually it was as cut and dried a thing as any hardware deal you've ever made. The fact remains, though, that as a younger woman I was in the dark about a mighty lot of things for a mighty long time. All women used to be.' For a moment it seemed that she had finished speaking and that no one would say anything more. There was the gentle lapping sound of the lake down at the beach and faint music from a radio somewhere in the neighborhood. But presently my stepmother spoke again. Her voice drowned out those indistinct murmurings I had been listening to, but while she spoke I felt a similar sensation in my ear. 'I had been in Italy a year and a half when I was a young lady,' she said, 'yet it never occurred to me that any husband in St. Louis, Missouri, might really be keeping a ladylove down the block. I thought all those things were customs of foreign countries.'

My father glanced warily at me and all of a sudden became preoccupied with two sailboats out on the lake. His wife with equal suddenness gave way to irrepressible and infectious laughter. 'Do you think, Gerald,' she said, 'that our boy here misses a single trick?' Then looking at me she spoke in an alto voice that I recognized as imitative of my own. 'Anyhow, he probably knows twice as much as his old man.' I tried to give a knowing look, because I thought it was expected of me. Then I saw my father turn his blue eyes from the lake to her with a smile that was submissive. At such moments it seemed that she meant to him exactly what she meant to me, and that without her we might now be sitting together on the porch of some summer hotel looking dumbly at the strangers about us. It was mid-morning, and springing up in a burst of energy, I challenged my father to a swim in the lake.

The house at Harbor Point was known as the Cottage. I had been surprised on my arrival to find that it was not a cottage at all but a long rambling clapboard house. It was a very big house indeed, yet everything there contrasted with the dark paneling and the stained-glass windows of the house in St. Louis. Outside, the clapboard walls were painted white and the roof was painted a bright blue. I liked to wander off down the beach and look back at the house and see my father and stepmother sitting on the porch or in the white chairs on the lawn near the sundial.

The memorable thing about the whole summer was Father's unbroken gay spirits and Mother's complete happiness. After the first week or so they quit having so much company, and Father worked on the lawn with the chauffeur and me. The chauffeur taught Father to sail, and he and Mother and I would spend whole days out on the lake. Mother even conceived the notion of having a late vegetable garden and staying on through September. Mother and Father planted the garden together and the two of them worked it. Sometimes Father would have to make hurried business trips to St. Louis, and when he returned the first thing he wanted to know was how the garden was doing. Mother said that their simple life was the talk of the whole summer colony; she said that for the benefit of the neighbors she ought to change the name of the Cottage to the *Petit Trianon* and build a 'Temple of Love' at the far end of the garden.

Late in August Father made one of his trips to St. Louis, and the second day after he left we had a letter from him saying that Mr. Tom Colby had died at his desk the day before and that the board of directors had named Father acting president. The letter arrived during the morning. My stepmother was in the living room with me, coaching me in my French make-up lessons. She read the letter aloud. Then, folding the paper, she kissed it before returning it to the envelope and said with a breathless little laugh, 'Tout est fini, mon fils.'

'You mean for Mr. Colby?' I said.

'No, for the garden, I suppose.' Then she pretended to frown at me, saying, 'There you go, letting me talk in that romantic, girlish way again.'

But at that moment it seemed very natural for my stepmother to talk in that girlish way, because during that moment it seemed to me that she was a girl. She seemed a girl to me, yet I did not relate her age to my own. I merely saw her as a young woman in love with my own father, who was ageless. It was not a permanent change of my view, it was only the impression of a moment; a second later I saw her reach forward to the cigarette box on the coffee table and saw her light the first cigarette I had ever known her to smoke. Perhaps it was her first. She inhaled, I observed, and she didn't cough; but she held the cigarette awkwardly between her thumb and forefinger. For a minute she appeared to me as a woman of an undecided, wicked age, baffling to itself. Perhaps it was only the cigarette, because when she had snuffed it out in the metal tray she was my own beloved Mother again, almost roly-poly, only a little too tall and too dignified for that.

Instead of feeling estranged from her, I felt that some miracle had now made her my real mother.

She was sitting quite straight on the couch with her hands folded in her lap. I was not even sure that she had really smoked the cigarette; it seemed too improbable, for now she seemed to me just the kind of woman that you wouldn't connect with smoking or with anything like that. While I sat gazing at her she turned to me quickly and said, 'I'm forty-two, Quint, if that's what you want to know.' We laughed spontaneously and congenially. 'It's wonderful to have a son,' she said. 'I always knew it would be such fun to say things like that to him.'

I blushed, and then with sudden self-assurance I teased her, saying, 'Oh, you don't like having a boy.' Presently she had become preoccupied with her own thoughts, but I insisted, 'You can't fool me.'

'My boy,' she said, 'you don't know.' She looked straight into my eyes. 'I wanted a son so awfully, Quint, in my first marriage.'

'Did *he*?' I asked. And I was surprised at my own question.

'Did . . . ?' She was obviously as surprised as I was.

'Did Mr. Lauterbach?' I felt myself blushing again. But I could see that she was pleased that I had asked and was glad to talk about it.

'When Carl Lauterbach and I were first married we used to talk about having a big family of boys and girls. I suppose I wanted a boy more than he did; I don't suppose he cared as much about having a child of any sort as I thought he did. A big family was merely another of the luxuries that we knew we could afford. When we married we had each just come into a family fortune, and the sky seemed the limit in anything.'

'Had you always known him?' I asked.

'No, I hadn't. I was away from St. Louis so much when I was in my teens. And then too, the Lauterbachs—well, Papa and everybody used to speak of them as 'beer people.' But Papa liked Carl. We were engaged before Papa died. Carl was a very dashing young man whom everybody liked.'

'I'd wondered about him,' I said.

'There's not much to tell, son, really. The main trouble, I suppose, was that he continued to be 'dashing.' He didn't want to get old. And in a sense I did want to. We were having our troubles even before my second girl was born, but he used to complain that after my second baby was a girl I began treating him like a little boy. Carl wanted a family, but he wanted other things too. We weren't happy together very long.'

'I'm sorry,' I said, lowering my eyes.

'You mustn't be sorry,' she said. 'Or else we wouldn't be here now.'

'I'm not really sorry!'

Again we burst out laughing, but not quite so spontaneously. After a moment she said absent-mindedly, 'We must start packing up—lock, stock, and barrel.' Her words had no literal meaning but they did express a finality which Father's letter had given to that morning. And I was wild to get back to St. Louis and even to

Country Day School, which I had hated. Already I could see myself standing among the boys in their cashmere sweaters and low-quarter tennis shoes, speaking of her for the first time outside the family as my mother.

The girls went East to school that winter, but they came home for Thanksgiving and Christmas; they even came one week end before Thanksgiving. So it hardly seemed that they were gone at all. While they were away, there were dinner parties and evenings of cards when the voices of men and women down in the library and drawing room could be heard all the way up to the third floor. When the girls were in town the whole house was noisy with the voices of young people. They would bring home with them visitors who lived in Omaha and East Orange, and a party had to be given in honor of each guest. I always met their trains with the German chauffeur, riding with him in the front seat of the limousine, and saw them to the station at the end of each visit. I would look at the map sometimes and be impressed by the idea of their traveling the distance from St. Louis to New York so many times with so little thought of it. But I was impressed still more by a thing that had happened to me at the Country Day School, although, come to think of it, I wasn't certain whether it had happened to me at school or at home.

My full name was Quintus Cincinnatus Lovell Dudley. Letters from my grandmother always had that long name of mine on the envelope, written in her large, clear script. My stepsisters sometimes saw these letters, and then they would call me Cincinnatus or Lovell and begin imitating my Tennessee drawl. Whenever their mother overheard them she did not hesitate to remind them that mine was an aristocratic name and that their surname would forever be linked with the beer that had made their paternal grandfather's fortune. There was never any resentment of her reminder, however, for Laura and Bess said they were too sensible to be ashamed of their origin. Laura would lament, 'Snubbed again by the Old Nobility.' And they would put their heads together and harmonize on the brewery's commercial theme song:

> *Serve it bottled or on draught,*
> *With your meals, before, and aft.*
> *Drink it dark, or drink it light,*
> *But drink your Lauterbach tonight.*

It was one of Bess Lauterbach's beaus in the Upper School at Country Day who heard the girls call me Cincinnatus. Then it happened that I was passing out of chapel one morning when this fellow put his hand on my shoulder and said, 'How's Cincinnatus?' I withdrew instantly and stared up at the offender. I very nearly found myself saying, 'Bess says you're too young for her,' because that was the judgment she had passed on him. Instead, I began to try to slip away from him through the crowd. I had moved through the doorway into the porch when I heard Freddy Todd saying, 'What's the hurry, Cincinnatus? Don't you like your own name, Cincinnatus?' By the end of that day it seemed that everyone in my class had called me 'Cinci-nottus' or merely 'Cincy' or 'Old Nat.' I was miserable.

Next morning I waited by the drug store, dreading the sight of the Special. When the other boys who boarded it at the same corner arrived, I went inside the drug store and pretended to look at the magazines. I bought a copy of *College Humor* and two Baby Ruths. It occurred to me that I had enough money to ride the regular streetcar and that by doing so I could put off the time when they would begin teasing me again about my name. Through the glass door I saw the Special arrive and saw the boys peering out the windows. I felt that they were looking for me; I stepped back to the druggist's counter and asked for a box of cough drops. I was told that cough drops should be purchased at the candy counter. When I returned to the door, the Special was still waiting for the traffic light to change. I was suddenly struck with my own foolishness, and opening the door, I ran out onto the sidewalk and into the street, calling to the conductor, 'Special . . . Special . . . Special.' But the streetcar moved off with the traffic. Some of the boys in the back end of the car saw me; they waved and laughed and shouted:

'Quintuscincinottus . . . Quintoscincinottusquintocinci . . . Notasquintocinci. . . .'

I had to transfer twice on the regular lines, and I soon realized that I was going to be over an hour late to school. I had the scolding of the masters to dread now, as well as the teasing about my name. I began to analyze myself and my situation and wondered why on earth I had ever wanted to continue at the same school for two years and give up the peace of being nobody. I cursed whatever it was in me that had made me want to be known. I kept hearing the sound of my ridiculous name as the boys had called it from the streetcar; then something made me think of Grandma's farm in Tennessee and the summers I had spent there with my cousins—cousins who could repeat my full name without a smile. I could hear them calling me out on the lawn the night I left Tennessee for the last time. It was the summer before Father had married my stepmother, and he had arrived that afternoon to take me back to St. Louis. Grandma must have known what was about to take place. I suspect that she had had more than one letter from him about his plans, but all day long she kept asking, 'What can possess the man? Taking the boy to the Middle West in this heat!' And it was not merely an outward show that she made to the family and to Aunt Muncie in the kitchen. She talked to them and she talked to me and even to the other grandchildren about it, expressing only the greatest wonder and bafflement, but also when I was cleaning my white shoes on the kitchen stoop that morning, I heard Grandma out at the cis-

tern mumbling to herself, asking herself the same foolish, rhetorical question: 'What can possess the man?'
During the afternoon when I was already dressed in
my white ducks and had my blazer on a coat hanger in
the side hall, I sat in one of the wobbly old wicker
chairs under the trees and watched her coming and
going from the house to the chicken yard and to the
arbor and the milk shed, where she had Aunt Muncie's worthless-boy cleaning up things. She wouldn't
let me or anybody else from the family help her that
day. Yet she wasn't still a minute. She couldn't stay in
the house, and it seemed that all outdoors was hardly
room enough for her to move around in. After a while
I saw her go down through the old abandoned formal
garden toward the springhouse to get a jar of something she had left there to cool; and presently she
came up the slope again carrying the jar. Just before
she reached the house, she stopped, and I heard her
say, 'Pshaw!' I knew from past experience what had
happened. She had forgotten to snap the padlock on
the springhouse door and was afraid the little Negroes
would be in there playing in the water. Without even
asking her, I jumped up and ran down through the old
garden toward the springhouse.

As I neared the little stone house, set halfway in the
side of the hill, I noticed that the heavy batten door was
being drawn to. The little Negroes were already there!
I stooped and picked up a handful of pebbles; then
I ran to the springhouse and threw open the door.

Inside I saw nothing but a small piece of wood whittled into the shape of a rowboat, floating in the spring water. But I knew that the Negro boys must be there, concealed in the darkness. In another second I heard them breathing, and I realized that they were standing flat against the opposite wall. I began to hurl my pebbles one at a time, and only by the sound the pebbles made could I tell when I hit the invisible targets. Suddenly it occurred to me that they were like gray squirrels against the bark of a tree; the very idea made me hesitate a moment.

And they were ready to seize the moment. They came splashing and whooping across the pool of water toward me! In consternation I fell back and let them make their escape. They ran along the back lane, their bare brown backs glistening in the sun, still whooping and yelling in their shrill voices. I watched them until they were out of sight, and then I turned back to the open doorway. Stepping into the springhouse, I sat down on the edge of the cased-up water and tried to reach for the little boat, which I considered my rightful booty, but it had drifted beyond my reach. I sat there thinking that if I reported the Negroes for wading in the spring, Grandma would only laugh and say, 'Why, those black little rascals! I ought not to have forgotten that door.' Yet if she heard of my wading in the spring she would certainly punish me and report it to my father. Even Rob and Jeff had rules against wading in the spring, and they would have only contempt for me if I put my foot in the water.

Yet all at once I wished not that I were like Rob and Jeff but like the kinky-headed Negroes that you could not see against the wall. I wished that I were like the barbarous Indians who came and murdered the children and then fell on their bellies by the creek and drank. I began taking off my shoes and socks. It would seem worth while living in the country if you were black or brown or red. But if you were white at all, even if you cared only for the little Confederates or the Indian children, that was too much. You must lie in wait for the old white woman, and when she has forgotten to lock the door, you must dash in and cool your black feet in the drinking water. I had removed my second sock and was pushing myself up from the rock floor when the shadow from the doorway fell across my white foot.

I turned around . . . and it was Father there at the door. He said nothing, and he did not appear to be angry. He took me by one of my hands, while with the other I reached down and gathered up my shoes and socks. As he led me up through the garden with its broken urns and untrimmed hedges, I saw Grandma standing at the gate nearest the house. She was pulling off her work gloves and wiping her face on her sleeve. Before we reached the upper end of the garden, she turned and went slowly toward the house. But even before Father began to talk I felt that the rest of my life my grandmother would be a retreating figure like that for me. This had been her last stand in the old warfare between them, and in reality her puttering and ordering and foolish questioning this day had been only for the purpose of covering her retreat.

As we came through the garden, she moved toward the house, and when she had entered the back door, I turned my eyes to my father, whose face seemed flushed with victory. He was saying that he wanted me to go back to St. Louis with him to meet a new friend of his—'A poor widow-woman,' he said, 'with two beautiful daughters.'

I didn't understand at first. 'Is she really very poor?' I asked.

'Oh, not really,' he said rather shyly. 'She's really a woman of means.'

'Then she *isn't* poor?' For a moment I caught a glimpse of Grandma standing at one of the upstairs windows in the ell of the house.

'She's a very rich woman, son.' Afterward I always remembered the mental picture I formed at that moment. Probably I remembered it because it was so outlandishly false. I imagined a corpulent little woman dressed in black (because she was a widow—it was only later, from her own lips, that I learned she was a divorcee; Father didn't tell me that, though I imagine he told my grandmother) with an absurdly round, ruddy, pockmarked face; sandy blonde hair worn in a kinky bob; plump, freckled arms; and stubby fingers loaded with diamonds (because she was rich). 'She would not consent to marry me,' Father said with a coyness that seemed strange in him, 'until her own children—the two beautiful daughters—gave their permission. She said all along that it had to be their decision. And so I guess *I* had better ask *your* permission, old man.'

'Yess'r,' I said—too quickly, I knew. But I knew too that what I was saying didn't make much sense in any case, and didn't matter. I glanced back at the house to see if Grandma was still standing at the window, but by then we had rounded the barn lot and I couldn't see that end of the house.

That night Grandma and Father sat apart from my uncles and aunts and the other grown people on the porch. I lay flat on the wide stone wall that ran from the porch to the cistern and heard their voices humming intermittently like the katydids and jar-flies that seemed to answer one another in the dark from away off in the garden. From off toward the greenhouse I could hear the cries of a rain crow. I lay gazing at the lightning bugs, wondering why they all seemed to move upward, why none of the lights came downward. Off at the far end of the porch beyond the thick masses of the magnolia tree the other children were playing their night games, and I could hear them asking now and again:

'Where is Quint?'

'Where is old Quintus?'

'Where do you reckon Quint is?'

Finally they began to call me. The boys went out into the shadowy recesses of the lawn, calling my name among the trees. Once they made a chorus of their high voices and called my full name, 'Quintus

Cincinnatus Lovell Dudley!' Later the girls wandered through the big halls and rooms of the ell-shaped house, all calling:

'Quintus . . . Quintus . . . Quintus . . . Quintus.'

I lay on the stone wall with my face turned toward my father, who had stopped talking to Grandma now and had stopped rocking his chair. Through the sweet-scented dark air I could feel my father's eyes. I thought that I could almost feel their light blue color. It was Father's eyes that seemed to arrest me and paralyze me there. They forbade me to move so much as the little finger of my hand, and I had no voice to answer the children. Lying on the wall, I could barely remember what had happened at the springhouse that day or what had happened during any of the summers I had spent at the farm; and the children wandering out in the yard and through the house were utter strangers to me and seemed a hundred miles away. Already I could feel the motion of the train carrying me away, to nowhere. I felt that I was nobody and nothing and that I did not exist and that all the decisions that the rich widow and her daughters and my father might make could not affect me. And then, as I lay there, I recalled a picture of a Chinese city in my geography book and the caption under it: *What Happens in China Affects* YOU. We were going to St. Louis that night; we were taking the Midnight; we would be there in the morning if the switchman in Evansville made no mistake.

The second period was almost over when I finally got to school. And it was just my luck that the headmaster was visiting in my study hall when I reported. 'I missed the Special, sir,' I said to the master in charge.

The master glanced at his wristwatch and then looked at the headmaster. Presently he turned to me. 'The second period is nearly over. Go to your desk, Dudley, and expect to see your name on the list for Saturday Session.'

'Yes, sir.' The headmaster's eyes were fixed on me, and I felt myself trembling as I turned away. But I was congratulating myself upon having gotten off light when the headmaster, who spoke with a stammer, halted me:

'J-just a minute, son. . . . What's . . . wh-what's the boy's name?' he asked the master.

'Dudley. Quintus Dudley.'

'Aren't you Anna Lauterbach's boy. . . ? A-a-anna Dudley, that is.'

'Yes, sir—yes, sir—yes, sir,' I answered in foolish, quick succession.

The headmaster, still rather flustered over the confusion of my stepmother's name, smiled amiably and recalled her maiden name. 'Anna Barnes she was, as a girl.'

'Yes, sir—yes, sir,' I repeated, reddening in my eagerness.

'Then you can't be such a b-b-bad boy.' Addressing the master he said, 'My s-s-sister and the boy's m-mother were schoolmates.'

The master smiled automatically and raised his blond eyebrows. 'Oh, indeed, is that so?'

'D-does this missing the Special happen often?'

'This is his first offense. Quint's a pretty darned decent fellow.'

My heart leapt to my throat. I believed for a moment that I would not even have to attend the Saturday Session.

'Well,' the headmaster continued in the same good-humored vein, 'there has to be a f-first time for everything—even S-saturday Sessions, even f-f-f-f-f-for Anna Barnes's boy.'

I went to my desk and forgot the headmaster and forgot the Saturday Session. I forgot the pain that the heckling about my name had caused me and ceased to dread future heckling. It was as though my stepmother had come to me in the midst of my difficulties. I took no real pride in having the headmaster know her, and after the first moment I didn't care at all about any advantages that the acquaintance might give me. For this was the grand realization of my summer's dream. In a sense this was the moment at which I had come into practical possession of a mother. I thought of the peculiar happiness of loving her as I did, and I thought of the firmness with which I was established in her heart. Suddenly I had become the carefree hero of a wonderful adventure, and I was ready to have all the fun of it. It seemed that she had given me the power to breathe and that she was at the same time the breath and the air breathed. And just as it is not necessary to remember to breathe in the midst of a foot race, from that day forward mere thoughts about her would become too tedious for me to bother with.

When the headmaster began to leave, the master followed him to the door. The study hall was about half full of boys, who had been watching me ever since I arrived. While the master's back was turned, Freddy Todd slipped me a note. 'You missed the Special on purpose. I saw you in the drug. F.T.'

I turned the note over and wrote on the back of it, 'You bet yr. boots I did.' I felt my own boldness. 'You ought to see the new issue of *College Humor* I bought.' And then striking what was probably the first note of irony of my life, I wrote, 'Please don't tell my mama.' To this I added one final stroke by signing the note, 'Q.C.L.D.'

The master had now followed the headmaster into the hall. When the door closed behind them, I raised the lid to my desk and banged it down six times to the rhythm of 'Shave-and-a-hair-cut . . . two bits.' A roar of laughter filled the study hall, and the master hurriedly re-entered. In the hush that fell over the room I sat with half a Baby Ruth crammed into my mouth and a solemn expression on my face. I opened my French grammar and purposely held it before me upside down.

When the girls came for Thanksgiving, Laura had a great boil-like pimple on the side of her nose and another, slightly smaller, on her chin. In the railroad station yard she held her handkerchief over the lower

71

half of her face and hurried out through the depot to the car, leaving Bess and their visitor from Omaha to identify the luggage. The dismayed chauffeur, cap in hand, turned first to follow Miss Laura, then turned back to Miss Bess, and then toward Miss Laura again. Equally dismayed, I simply watched the tall chauffeur's turnings. 'Gus!' Bess called as the poor man started away; and he returned immediately. Then to me she said, 'Laura isn't well. Why don't you run wait with her in the car?'

I whirled about and ran through the enormous lobby, dodging between the groups of travelers and once hurdling a large suitcase. I ran two-steps-at-a-time up the wide flight that led to the main entrance and joined Laura just inside the doorway. Hearing my commotion, she turned around, and in her surprise and confusion she no longer held the handkerchief to her face. I saw her pimples now for the first time and said in a loud, high-pitched voice, 'Bess said you were sick. Did she only mean those places?'

Instantly, almost before Laura's face flushed, the thought of what I had said made me feel sort of sick all over. I had spoken to her as though she were just another child; and Laura was a young lady now. She wore heels that were even higher than her mother's, but the real mark of young-ladyhood for me was the wide leopardskin collar on her dark coat. Her black hair, heavy as her mother's but more wiry, was worn in a short, curly, almost tangled bob that resembled a Russian cap. When she had got off the train she was carrying her hat, as she nearly always did, instead of wearing it. Standing at the top of the wide flight, she still held the black hat in one hand and her white handkerchief in the other. When I spoke out in my loud, nervous voice, a deep pink suffused her unhappy countenance—a blush that momentarily hid her blemishes—and I felt that she was looking for someone over my shoulder. I glanced over my shoulder at the crowd. It seemed to me that every eye in the vast domed waiting room was fixed upon Laura at the top of those steps. Then I watched her as she stood a moment staring boldly back at the crowd. Presently she brought her handkerchief up to her face again and hurried through the revolving door.

It was snowing and it had turned dark since I went inside. I had to think a moment to remember where the limousine was parked. 'Where's the car?' Laura asked.

'It's—oh, it's down yonder,' and I led the way along the wall of the stone depot. Laura began to laugh, and she said:

'I'd forgotten what a little Rebel you-all are.'

I opened the door for her to get in the back seat of the limousine and I climbed into the front. I slid back the glass division and said, 'Laura, I'm sorry I shouted so. I was all scared about your being sick.'

'That's all right,' she said. 'I was only afraid there might be somebody or other in the station. But there was nobody.'

'Were you looking for somebody?'

'I should say not! And there wasn't anybody. I looked over the whole crowd, and there wasn't a soul there. I didn't want to be seen by anybody in this condition, and usually you do run into people at the station during the holidays. But I was in luck. There wasn't a soul, young or old.'

When Bess and the visitor joined us, Laura asked, 'Did you see anybody at all in the station?'

'Nobody at all,' Bess said. 'We must have been the only people coming in.'

But the visitor from Omaha said, 'Why, I thought I saw a couple of thousand people in the lobby.'

Laura and Bess laughed heartily, and I joined in.

'You know what I mean,' Bess explained soberly. 'Anybody you'd know.' And we all laughed again. It was snowing harder now. The car moved slowly along, and the windshield wipers made two black arcs on the snow-covered glass in front of me.

Laura did not appear at dinner that night. She had slipped in the back door of the house and up the service stairs to her room. There she greeted Mother, but I did not see her again. And when the family sat down to dinner, my father was still asking if Laura had not asked to see him, if he could not just run up to her room and say hello, if she were really feeling pretty bad?

'She's not feeling bad at all,' Bess said. 'But she's taken an oath that no man shall put eyes on her till that ivory complexion is restored.'

'She's a perfect nut,' Mother said. 'Elsa,' she addressed the maid who was moving around the table in a pair of squeaky black shoes, 'Miss Laura wants her dinner in her room. See that she gets nothing very solid. A cup of this bouillon and a glass of Bulgarian milk should do a sick girl—with some dry toast.'

'Mother,' Bess said sourly, 'what a heartless view you take!'

'Not at all. A light diet will probably cure what ails her.'

'Let us not kid one another, dearest Mother.'

'What do you think, Alice?' Mother asked the visitor from Omaha.

'You've got a sure cure, Mrs. Dudley,' Alice said. Turning to Father she said, 'If she sticks to that diet, Laura will be hale and hearty and down to breakfast in the morn, eh, Mr. Dudley? Don't you think so?'

Father had kept his eyes on Mother's face. Slowly he moved them now to the plain-spoken visitor and nodded his head in silence.

'They talk about Victorian mothers!' Bess exclaimed. 'Go ahead! Starve her out, M'ma! It's your house and your food!'

All eyes were suddenly upon Bess, and every face, except hers—even mine—had reddened slightly. There was certainly not the slightest tint in her own ivory complexion. She took up her knife and fork and began to cut the white sole.

When the plump little maid pushed open the polished swinging door again, my stepmother said, 'Elsa, see that Miss Laura has some of everything. . . . Tell

Cook the potatoes are quite good this way, Elsa. . . . See that Miss Laura has enough potatoes with her sole.'

After dinner Father played rotation with Bess and Alice and me. Mother went upstairs for another consultation with Laura. As she left the billiard room she said to Father, whose eyes had followed her to the doorway, 'I know she'll be wanting to see her old father after a while.'

'I hope so,' he said rather dolefully. During the game that followed he was noticeably silent. Bess was even more noticeably talkative. Father spoke only now and then to ask some question about Laura's ailment. As his silence seemed to deepen, Bess's talk became noisy and capricious. At first she tried to amuse him by telling anecdotes about things that happened during her week ends in New York. 'Oh, you should have seen us that day!' she said, and I tried to listen to what she said. But it was hard somehow to keep my mind on it. Her silly exclamations seemed to make more sense to me than the stories she was telling. 'Oh, we were a scream!' Everything she mentioned seemed so abstract and unfamiliar: Fifty-seventh Street, Columbus Circle, Central Park. Whenever Father did look up from the table at her, there was a vague look in his eyes as though these stories didn't interest him either. 'Gosh, it was too, too funny, really!' But none of it seemed funny or important the way her stories about St. Louis did. 'And so Buddy came up to Nan in the Plaza lobby,' she was saying, 'looking like he had lost his last rattle. "I guess this is really good-by," he moaned. Nan only looked at him worshipfully without saying word one. So then I put in my two cents' worth. "Buddy," says I, "if the elopement's all off, are you going back to New Haven, after all?" Buddy set his jaw out like this and said, "Yeah, damn it. I'll get my diploma and go back to Cleveland. I'll go back and get married and have three swell kids and go down hill fast as hell!"'

Alice threw back her head and rocked with laughter. 'It's grand the way you tell it, Bess,' she gasped, 'but you really have to know those two dopes to get the beauty of it.'

Here Father interrupted. He asked, 'When did Laura's face start breaking out? Has she been feeling bad lately? Generally, I mean.'

'She feels grand, but when we were packing our bags yesterday those bumps began to swell, poor girl. On the train I told the porter she had measles. She made him leave her berth down all the way out today, and I played cards with her.' And Bess continued to tell one story after another, all of them ending with some joke she had made or something clever she had to say about the episode. Before their dates arrived I had said to myself: How independent she is! How smart she is!

At last Father had ceased to look up even when she said, 'Listen!' or 'This is *too* good!' And now her voice got louder and louder until it reverberated in the vaulted ceiling and filled the room. Father now seemed

77

to take even greater pains with his game, leaning across the table or standing back to eye the position of the number three ball. And he watched with a critical or an approving eye the shots that the others made. But I was, on the contrary, able to show little interest in the game. When my turn came round I found myself staring at Bess, and I had to ask what was the lowest number on the table. She laughed at me, insisted at first that I must forfeit my shot, then said that she would give me to the count of ten to find the correct number; and she ended by prodding me in the ribs with her cue. In the midst of our horseplay Father asked, 'Just to what extent *is* Laura's face broken out?'

I was watching Bess when the question came. I glanced at my father and then turned back to my stepsister. 'Heavenly days!' she said. I looked at Father again. His intent blue eyes questioned: What do you mean? How dare you speak so to your elder?

Bess's direct gaze replied: There's a limit to all patience! More than her gaze (for there was really little expression in her eyes) her widespread mouth and her raised eyebrows said this. Her face very often expressed some superior feeling. I had always thought of it as her form of humor. Suddenly I laughed. But my throat was full of phlegm, and my sensation was the same I had had when I shouted to Laura at the top of the steps in the station.

After a moment Bess said, 'Laura's going to be all right. Let us not fret, Father-chum.' And now you could tell from the way she tried to see herself in the glass covering her grandpapa's picture (an enlarged photograph of her mother's papa, taken on the Mediterranean with a big fish he caught there) and I knew by the way she pushed at her hair that she was wishing her date would arrive. Her hair, darker than Laura's even and without any curl, was cut in a severe Dutch bob. Tonight she wore a white flower near her left temple. Her shoulders were stooped, markedly so in this low-backed evening dress, and as she turned from the glass she straightened her shoulders self-consciously and tried to draw in her chin, which was almost as pointed as her grandpapa's white imperial.

When Mother returned to the billiard room, Bess and her visitor had already been called for. They had wrapped themselves in their velvet capes, their voices had sounded crisp and thrilling in the hall for a moment, and then the heavy front door had slammed. I listened in vain for the sound of their voices outside; in the big silent house I could hear only the soft tread of my stepmother on the stairs. The sudden crack of the pool balls thoroughly startled me, and I turned to see my father still bent over the table but watching expectantly for his wife—or for Laura?—in the doorway.

'Are ladies allowed in here?' Mother asked at the door. When my father gave no answering smile, I put on a tough face and said: 'It's okay, Miss, if you won't mind the cussin'.'

'It's blankety-blank all right with me,' she said. She sat down on a straight chair by the door and looked at

Father. 'Is it blankety-blank all right with you, Mr. Dudley?'

'How's Laura feeling, Ann?' he said. He was putting away his cue. 'She still doesn't want me to see her, I suppose.' He came and sat on the couch beside me. 'I shouldn't keep asking, but I don't get it.'

'It's just her terrible little vanity,' she said absently. She was bent forward to examine a snag in my sweater.

'I'm afraid I annoyed Bess,' Father said. 'I kept asking about Laura, and she lost patience with me. She wanted to talk about other things, I guess.'

'Oh, her terrible little ego too!' She reached forward and smoothed the loose threads of the sweater. 'Dear, sweet Gerald,' she said, looking at Father now, 'you mustn't let yourself be hurt by those girls of mine. You mustn't.'

'I like to think of them as my own girls,' he said.

It was as though it had taken this to get her complete attention. 'How can you,' she asked, straightening in her chair, 'when they've never even been quite mine, really?'

Again the blueness of my father's eyes asked: What do you mean? Glancing at me he said, 'You'd better get upstairs to your lessons, Quint.'

I moved toward the door, but my stepmother put out her arm and encircled my waist. 'They're my own dear little girls, of course,' she said, 'even if they have no thought of anyone but themselves. But what control have I over them?'

'Why, you're their mother, Ann.'

'They write their own checks, however.'

'Their checks?'

'You know they have their own money, Gerald.'

'Of course they do.'

'And they come and go at will.'

'My God, Ann! That's not everything, money.'

'No, it's not, Gerald.'

Father came and was drawing her arm from around me and pushing me toward the door. She waved to me clownishly as I went out. On the stairs I could still hear her voice, and it was not her normal speaking voice.

It seemed that nothing of any importance had happened tonight; the family was just as it had been before the girls' train arrived this afternoon; and yet I found myself wondering if it would always be the same. I wondered if it were possible that anything could ever make the girls not like to play rotation with Father and not want to tell him about the things they did, or if it were conceivable that Father would get so he didn't want to listen to their talk. I wondered if after a while the girls would not think I was a 'simply adorable little Rebel,' or if I would not care what they thought. What if my father and my stepmother should have a terrible quarrel? Would it be possible for them to? Could anything in the world make my stepmother stop loving my father or me? *Me?* If so, I wished I could get sick and die, and be dead when it happened. How could I want to live, what would be the point, what sense would anything make?

But when I reached the second floor I heard Laura's phonograph playing and laughed at myself. I felt foolish in quite the same way I had felt foolish once before, when I mistook the cushions of the pool table for a corpse. I began to climb the steps to my room on the third floor. I could hear Laura singing to the phonograph music. Laura was always in good spirits even when she was alone, I thought. I wanted to be like that, and so I ceased to worry about the family. There were things at school I had to think about, not my lessons but a new club and getting a name for it and whether or not they were going to make me vice-president of it.

Before Laura went back to school, Mother did make her consult a doctor, who finally decided that she was allergic to cheese and to tapioca.

At Christmas a ten-foot cedar tree was set up in the front hall. It was placed in a corner opposite the stairs, but its lower branches extended almost to the center of the hall. These branches had to be trimmed and a special base had to be constructed to make the tree stand erect. I watched Gus and old Herman, the butler, at work on the tree through an entire afternoon. Herman was afraid that the tree would fall on him or across some piece of furniture. He kept saying, 'Watch it, Gus! Watch it, now!' And Gus would sometimes wink at me, and exclaiming, 'Whoops!' he would allow the tree to fall slightly toward the old man. Then he would reach out his long arms just in time to catch the tree. Herman would jump backward, cover his bald head with his hands, and shout something in an Austrian dialect which Gus declared he could not understand. 'Speak English, man,' Gus would say, laughing and straightening the tree again. Finally Herman moved all the lamps and small pieces of furniture to the far end of the hall, and slipped on his white coat to show that he would have nothing more to do with the tree. 'What I've needed right along,' Gus declared, 'is the help of somebody who's a man yet. So give me a hand here, Quint.'

I stepped forward and said, 'Sure thing,' though I saw that the real job was already done. That night Mother and I decorated the tree. Last year Father and the girls had not only decorated the tree; they had gone to the country together and selected a tree that the farmer had not wanted to part with, and Father had come home complaining about how much it had cost him. But we all knew that his complaining was just his way of bragging about it. The next day he had brought home new sets of lights and ornaments and complained about how much they cost. But this year he said to Mother and me, 'It's your turn to see after the tree.' And he showed not the least interest in the project, although it was being carried out in honor of Laura and Bess—they were arriving from school the following day.

Gus and Herman brought the ladders up from the basement, and old Herman helped string the wires on the tree. My father was in the library going over some papers he had brought from the office that evening. Occasionally he would come to the doorway and watch us. Finally when his appearance became so regular that it was obvious he was pacing the floor of the library, Mother left off the work she was doing atop the ladder and said, 'Is our chatter disturbing you, Gerald?'

'I've got to run down to the office a while,' he said.

'Nonsense. This can wait till tomorrow. I'm sure Herman wants to be off tonight anyway. Be gone, Herman! And Quint ought to be studying. Get thee to thy books, boy!'

'No, it's not that at all.' Father was already passing through the hall to the coat closet under the stairs. 'I won't be gone an hour.'

Herman had not waited to hear the outcome of matters; by the time my father had pulled the side door softly behind him, I was alone with my stepmother, each of us sitting erect on the top rung of a stepladder close to the half-decorated cedar tree. I moved my foot as though I might be preparing to descend my ladder, but Mother told me to wait a minute.

'We can finish it early in the morning,' I said, knowing that we could not. 'Before I go to school Gus will be here, and he's more help than Herman.'

'It's something about the girls, don't you think?'

'I don't know, Mother. Let's stop for tonight.'

'Has he talked to you about them, son?'

'No. He's just been thinking about business a lot. He's always grouchy then.'

'You're more observant than that, Quint. It's about the girls.'

'They didn't pay enough attention to him at Thanksgiving, I think.'

'You're darned right they didn't.'

'But what does he expect?'

'Of them?' she asked. 'Do you think they're pretty snotty, Quint?'

'Oh, no, Mother. He wants everybody to like him and to be always showing him how much they do, or he isn't sure about them. He doesn't think anybody likes him really. and he doesn't like anybody much really except—'

'Except you.'

'And you.'

'Quint, I wonder if—'

'And the girls too, Mother. He likes Laura and Bess a lot . . . but for a reason.'

'How so, Quint?'

'They've helped him a lot, somehow.'

'You know, Quint, I've always been afraid he might like me for a reason.'

'I can't see why you think that. With you it's different.'

'I'm rich as all get out, Quint.'

'Pooh. I don't believe you're so rich.' I smiled at her.

But later I went up to my room on the third floor. I closed the door without even turning on the light; and throwing myself across the bed, I began to sob in my pillow. There were no tears, but for a long time I lay there sobbing. Finally I rolled over on my back, and with my dry eyes wide open in the dark I thought that I saw a vision of that corpulent, kinky-headed, bedizened widow whom I had pictured when Father first told me about the rich Mrs. Lauterbach.

The girls' Christmas holiday lasted for over two weeks. During this time Mother arranged three parties for them. The first was a luncheon at the Country Club, in honor of their visitor from East Orange. After the visitor had left us to visit other girls in Detroit and Cleveland and Chicago, there were two other parties—not at the Country Club but at home. My own holidays had begun by this time, and I hung around the house listening to the girls' talk or entertaining their beaux before they came down in the evening. For my father no longer lingered in the billiard room after dinner at night; he went upstairs with Mother or to the library with his brief case—several times he went to his office for an hour or so.

My sisters begged me to appear at both of the evening functions. Laura even said that she wanted me to sit on her right at the dinner part. And at the open-house they thought it would be 'too cunning' if I would stand with them in a receiving line. But I came downstairs for only a few minutes at each party, only long enough to get some refreshments and say hello to the people I knew. On the night of the open-house I sat for a while on the bottom step of the stairway, drinking punch. I watched Laura in conversation with a young man standing in the center of the drawing room, and it seemed that all the while her eyes kept darting about the room to see who was watching her. And I once saw Bess sitting at the grand piano, which was painted white and was partly covered by a dark shawl. She was striking chords thoughtfully while she and Letitia Jackson listed the girls who would probably make their debut with them next year. My stepmother said Bess had had piano lessons for three years and had never learned to play a single piece through.

The parties themselves interested me very little. But the preparations for them had so fascinated me that, during the week before, I could hardly tear myself away from the cook's and maid's talk in the kitchen to hear what Herman and Gus said about shifting pieces of furniture in the front rooms, or away from the girls' discussions of the guest list to hear my mother on the telephone ordering flowers. What interested me most of all, however, was the talk that Mother and Father had about the refreshments. The girls wanted to serve cocktails before the dinner and highballs at the open-house. Father was against it. Mother said that she opposed it in principle. The girls were too young for that sort of thing, and she felt that their debut year would be early enough to begin it. But she said that she would not forbid it if the girls should insist. 'Insist?' Father echoed. After that he would discuss the question no further.

About three o'clock in the afternoon before the dinner party Father's car stopped in front of the house. It was strange to see it there, since Father usually drove directly to the garage. I was in the side yard passing a football with Gus. For a moment I held the ball, feeling it inquisitively as though I were blindfolded and trying to identify an object. I watched Father move quickly up the steps and into the house. It gave me that same sensation which seeing a doctor enter the house always used to do.

I started to throw the ball to Gus. But Gus was now walking toward the rear of the house. 'Back to work, my boy,' he called to me.

'Take the ball,' I called after him with a certain desperation. But the lanky chauffeur was already out of sight. My impulse was to hurl the football away into the street or over the hedge into the next lawn. I stood there a moment, puzzled by my own feelings. Why had I wanted to throw the ball away? I couldn't understand it. During another moment I stood looking at the football; then tucking it under my arm, I ran toward the house.

My father's overcoat was thrown across a chair in the hall. His hat was hung over the newel post near the Christmas tree. I went up the stairs and found my stepsisters standing by the carved balustrade that guarded the huge stairwell. 'Why is Father home so early?' I asked them. The door to my stepmother's room was closed.

'He came to tell us he has to work tonight and can't make the party,' Bess told me.

Laura was smiling. 'But Mother says he doesn't have to work tonight and that he can make the party.'

As I continued to climb the stairs to the third floor, Bess said, 'You'd better stick around and hear the verdict.'

'What difference does it make?' I said casually.

'Difference to whom?' Bess said almost under her breath. I looked back over my shoulder.

I had now reached the third floor, but I heard very distinctly what Laura was saying: 'I know the story of another man who got so he didn't always come home in the evenings.'

A few minutes later from a window in the ballroom on the third floor I watched my father get into his car and drive down the street and out through the wide gateway of Portland Place.

I still had the football tucked under my left arm. I went down to the second floor and into Mother's room. She was seated on the bed, talking over the telephone to the groceryman who had failed to send the right sort of mints. While she talked her eyes were fastened on me. When she put down the receiver, she lowered her eyes to the counterpane. 'I'm just as mad as blue blazes, son,' she said.

'I don't blame you,' I said.

'And I'm utterly powerless.'

'Damn it,' I said. I set the football on her dressing table among the bottles and complexion brushes.

'Yes. Gosh damn it,' she said.

'Is it about the whisky?'

'No, not essentially. It's still Laura's behavior at Thanksgiving, I guess.'

On the day of the open-house Father called Mother on the telephone and said he had to go to New York. I heard her begging him. She took the call at the telephone on the landing. I felt that I could not endure the tone of her voice and I tried to get out of earshot. But wherever I went on the first floor her voice seemed to follow me. Finally I went back to the billiard room, shut the door, and turned on the radio at full-blast.

After a few minutes she opened the door and looked at me sitting there with my ear close to the loudspeaker. She entered; and when she had closed the door again, her face suddenly flushed and she said very loudly, 'Turn it off!' I obeyed instantly. 'Don't be a coward, Quint!' she said when the room was quiet.

'What do you mean, Mother?'

She sat down on the couch and asked me to come and sit beside her.

'What did he say, Mother?'

'He said he must go to New York this afternoon to see a member of the board.'

'What's the matter?'

'Why, child, it's your father's pride.'

'But . . .'

'What does he say? Why, Quint, they've discovered that Mr. Colby was either very foolish or was dishonest. And your father suggests that they may ask for his own resignation.'

'Why should that be?'

'It's inconceivable. And either he takes me for a fool or means to insult me.'

'But he may be worried about money and things, at that.'

'Why on earth should he worry about money while he has me?'

I felt myself blushing again. I wondered why she must say such things to me. There was nothing I could say; she seemed to be crazy when it came to money. But presently I saw a conciliating expression in her eyes. 'Don't worry, boy,' she said. 'All good families have their quarrels.'

Father came back from New York only two days before the girls had to return to school. He arrived on Sunday morning and was in the conservatory at the end of the dining room when I came down to breakfast. 'Well, good morning, old boy,' he called to me, and I saw right away a complete change in his spirits. When Mother and the girls came down he greeted them in an affectionate and conciliating manner. There would be no more business difficulties, Father announced, for the most powerful members of the board had agreed to stand by him. During the following two days the household seemed its old self. Father and the girls played pool and twice they went together for long walks in Forest Park. Only the family were present for dinner on the last evening, and toward the end of the meal our gaiety had a quality of hysteria about it. Afterward, when everybody was about to leave for the railroad station, I went to the closet under the stairs to get my coat, and it was while reaching in the darkness and feeling about for its familiar sheep-skin collar that I realized the special quality of our gaiety. When I met the family in the hall, a sudden fit of depression had come over me. In the automobile I sat on one of the little folding seats alongside my father, who kept teasing me, saying that I should not be so gloomy, that the girls would be back in February.

Laura and Bess waved good-by to us through the window of the Pullman car. I turned to join my parents; but Mother had already walked far along the platform toward the iron gate, and Father was walking rapidly after her. I soon overtook them, and we walked through the lobby and climbed the steps to the street level. When we were in the limousine again, Father spoke. 'It's too bad that the one occasion I've had to be in New York this year should come while the girls were out here.'

I waited for Mother to speak, but she only nodded. And by the changing lights that came through the car window I could make out that her face was turned away from him toward me. When we had ridden several blocks, he said, 'Aren't you feeling well, Ann?'

'Very well, thank you, Gerald.' She cleared her throat and gave an artificial little laugh. 'Only I'm not so easily reconciled to your New York trip as the girls were. I don't want that to slip your mind now that they're gone.'

'My God, Ann, must I prove to you the terrible shape my business is in?'

'Why, Gerald!' She repeated the artificial laughter.

'Money's not everything, is it, Gerald—to you? No, Gerald, you let your pride spoil the whole of Christmas for you and Quint and me. But you didn't spoil the girls' holiday, didn't affect it in the least. And they were quick to forgive you, because they don't give a tinker's damn. You gained absolutely nothing by leaving town. You got lonesome in New York and so decided you were wrong about the girls and hurried home in time to pretend nothing had happened.'

'Are you quite sure you're well?'

'Don't concern yourself further with my health.'

I sat with my face pressed to the car window. I felt that they—especially my father—had forgotten I was present, and the shock of hearing them speak so rudely to one another was hardly a stronger sensation than the feeling of discomfort that came over me. When the limousine had finally pulled into the porte-cochere, I began to dread the sight of my parents' faces. I stayed in the car until they had entered the side door of the house.

After a moment I followed them inside. They had gone directly upstairs, and I followed without stopping to remove my coat. Passing their room at the head of the stairs, I could hear my mother's voice rising and falling and sometimes breaking off like a voice on the radio when it is suddenly switched off. And I could hear my father still trying to reason with her. They had completely forgotten my existence; I moved down the hall and began to ascend the stairs to the third floor, and at the turn of the stairs—at exactly that point where I had once before forsaken family problems and had begun to think of things at school— those things at school again came into my mind; and I even began to think that what happened to my family was not as important to me this year as it had been last year. Some far-off day I should have money of my own, like Laura and Bess, and a house of my own.

I was thirteen that year and I had a pair of long trousers. They were only sailor pants, but they were long at any rate; and I wore them on every possible occasion. Sometimes when I had worn them four or five days in succession, Mother would send me back upstairs to change them before going to school.

At school all of the student body were divided into the Reds and the Whites. This year I had a regular position on the Reds' basketball team in the Middle School, and I felt that I had learned from personal observation that most Reds were morally, intellectually, and physically superior to most Whites. The Reds won the first three games of the basketball season and might have won all the rest had our center not been transferred (by the master in charge) to the Whites. After we lost our center, the victories were divided about evenly. As the season progressed, resentment among the Reds increased. Every defeat was attributed to the loss of our long-legged center; and every decision against us was laid to the master's favoritism. By the middle of the season hardly a game was played in which the

Reds were not penalized for some kind of foul. I joined in the grumbling and complaining. No one sympathized more than I when Fred Todd was put out of the game for fouling four times. And soon I was contributing to the whispered chorus before every game: 'Get 'em how you can, but get 'em.' I was in the midst of every huddle with my arms about the necks of my teammates. Sometimes as I stood with my arms entwined with those of the other boys and as I listened to the plans they made or even suggested a plan of my own, a wave of self-consciousness would sweep over me, a memory of times when I was a new boy somewhere, when I would have had no heart for this huddling and plotting, this close alliance and competition with other boys. Suddenly I would ask myself: What am I doing here? What are these strangers to me?—boys whose fathers and mothers went to school together, strangers rolling their r's and talking sometimes of things they had done together in the first grade or mentioning casually what colleges they would go to, self-assured, cocky, yet soft-headed boys already sentimental over Yale or Dartmouth or Princeton where their names were entered on the rolls the year they were born—what sense did my own fellowship and rivalry with them make? What did I care about the Reds and the Whites? Did I really care whether they ignored me or called out, 'Atta-boy, Cincy!' and 'Dudley for the Dartmouth Cup!'? Ah, yes, I cared and could not deny it to myself. More and more every day since the time Mother had first put her arm about my shoulders, still more since I had come to live in her house, most of all since the day she had said, 'Tout est fini' and had lit the cigarette and since I had ceased to marvel at our mutual dependence, always more and more until now when I had ceased to connect the two spheres of my existence. Now I did not simply care; I hungered for the mere sound of my name. I wanted to compete and to excel. And so the wave of self-consciousness would pass over me and away, and this new spirit would remain. I would dash out across the court waving my arms, shouting for the ball, 'Freddy! Freddy! Here! Here! Here!'

During the first week in February there came a big snow. The school pond and the creek froze over. There was no basketball that week; everyone skated or played hockey or went sledding on the hill behind the Lower School building. On Monday of the second week we began to play ball again. It was in the second quarter of that Monday's game that I heard my name called, for fouling. I heard the master's whistle and then could hardly believe my ears when I heard my own name: 'Dudley, holding—two shots!'

There was a great outcry from the Reds and much running about and furious slamming of rubber soles on the floor of the court. The captain of the Whites stepped forward to make the two free shots. But neither time did the ball sink into the basket. A cry of joy went up from the Reds, and during our next huddle the captain of the Reds whispered, 'Give it to 'em, Cincy.' And it was then that I realized that even the

Reds had thought I was holding, and holding on purpose. The captain's name was Peck Johnston. I looked
into Peck's innocent brown eyes, and the right eye
winked at me. My first impulse was to declare my
innocence; but this was the first time I had ever received one of Peck's approving winks. Peck was a hard
guy to make a friend of, and nobody could throw
away the chance. I returned the wink without thinking
again of my honesty. I could think only of my own
popularity, of what it would be like, of how I might
really win the Dartmouth Cup for the best-all-round-
boy in the Middle School. It didn't occur to me then to
consider: What am I doing here? What are these
strangers to me?

And yet sometimes when I was feeling myself most
wholeheartedly given over to this new life of mine,
someone would begin kidding me about my peculiar
pronunciation of certain words: 'Oh, gee, look at that
pretty red-headed gull,' or, 'Say, you want to bet a
dahm on this game?' or 'Gosh, we had a reeyull good
tahm.' Originally this had annoyed and embarrassed
me, but I was coming to see the advantage that could
be made of it. I began to see that it gave me an unique
personality, made me a *character*. Even the boys in the
Upper School began to recognize me as the boy with
the 'reeyull Southern accent.' For a while the whole
Middle School was so uniformly aware of my Southern origin that during chapel all faces turned toward
me whenever we sang a Negro spiritual or a so-called
Southern folk song. There was even a period when I

felt that tears might come to my eyes when I raised my voice to sing about the old Kentucky home or about old Virginny the-state-where-I-was-born. Sometimes when I talked about Tennessee I realized that I was imitating my father and repeating things he had said about Grandma's farm and the old times. If, for a moment, a cloud of self-contempt cast a shadow over my other feelings, the cloud soon passed away, and I basked in the glorious attention of my classmates. Most of the boys were properly amused by the pose I had assumed, but some few took a serious, romantic view of it. And I cared quite as much for the one kind of attention as for the other. Alone in my room I would, indeed, sometimes examine my own affectations rather indifferently; and as I considered all of this Southern business, I would wonder if the South really did exist, if there was any actual difference between the people of the two parts of the country. If there were not—and I usually told myself that there was not—then how did such myths come into being? Why did grown people invent such ideas and keep them alive? I knew too little of history to look for an explanation there, and besides, the whole thing did not seem very important to me.

Usually I would dismiss the subject without much thought. But one night, as I turned over in bed, a long train of early memories of the summers at Grandma Lovell's began to pass across my mind. I recalled how I had once wanted to be like my cousins there, just as I now tried to be like the boys at Country Day. And surely that life did seem remote, and the people of another race. But I could not determine whether or not it seemed so merely because that was the country and this was the city. I thought about this for a long while. Then I thought again of my old longings to be a farm boy like my cousins. I kept going back to that (though at first I could not say why). I recollected the shame I used to feel at my own failure and my last desperate longing to be like the little Negroes; the memory of it was a torture to me. More painful still was the memory that I had allowed that shame to turn me against my grandmother and to make me submit to being taken away from her forever. I knew that my father would have permitted me to live on the farm the year round if I had begged for it, but instead I had been eager to get away from it. I thought of the boy I might have been in the place where I was born, and it seemed that that was the boy I should have been. It seems ridiculous now, but the notion that I should have loved my grandmother as I actually loved my stepmother, and the whole idea of my own failure and guilt, and above all, the fantastic notions of the strong character that I might have developed, so disturbed and depressed me that I resolutely shut off my memory and persuaded myself that I was quite sleepy.

The following morning I refused to think about those things. Within a few days I had completely put them out of my head. Yet my pose as The Southerner was always afterward distasteful to me, and I tried to avoid the words that had made my friends laugh and say that my accent was the 'reeyull thing.' I refused to talk at all about Tennessee.

But I did not refuse to talk about other things. I talked so much that I used to wonder about it myself. I was not satisfied just to excel on the playgrounds and in the classroom. I wanted to be recognized as a wit and to express some original opinion on every subject. For a while this new passion deprived me of all self-consciousness; it was as though a great store of energy had suddenly been released from within me, and I never knew, myself, what undertaking it would prompt me to next.

Nearly every Friday night I stayed at school to attend Scout meeting. By February I had become a First Class Scout and had won eight Merit Badges: for metal work, bird study, safety, journalism, stalking, wood turning, and reptile study. I joined the music club and so ingratiated myself with the music teacher that I was given a prominent (feminine) role in the senior musical comedy. I helped to found a club whose main purpose was the exchange of art magazines among its members. It was called the Tom Swift Club, and each member had a different volume of the Tom Swift series with the pages glued together and a hole cut in the center for carrying cigarettes. If the member's volume happened to be *Tom Swift and His Motorcycle*, as mine was, then he was called 'Motorcycle' by the other club members. If it were *Tom Swift and His Airship*, as in the case of Fred Todd, he was called 'Airship.' I secretly edited a scandal sheet called *La Confidante*, and was acting at the same time as reporter from the Middle School for the weekly school paper. In short, when Class Day approached in February, my name was the first to be mentioned as candidate for the Dartmouth Cup. The only other candidate was a boy whose grades were a good deal better than mine, but it was so obvious that the award would be voted to me that my rival purposely got himself disqualified by cutting two study halls the week before election. On Class Day the headmaster announced in chapel that I had been elected the best-all-round-boy in the Middle School. My stepmother was present to see me receive the cup, and as I went down the aisle toward the platform I caught a glimpse of the back of her head in the front row. Somehow, the sight of her tight-fitting felt hat made me aware for the first time since I had known her of a feeling of annoyance and even of resentment against her. I wished that she were not there, that she were at home in Portland Place, that she had left me to receive the Dartmouth Cup alone. I was unable to explain this to myself, and when I had accepted the cup and turned to go down the steps from the platform, it occurred to me to make amends for the thought by handing her the cup here before the whole student body. I came down the steps and turned to the left, toward my stepmother, but when I looked into her face with its eager, earnest expression, again I felt that she was an intruder, that she was demanding the cup, and that it was not of my own will that I was about to give it to her. I raised my eyes to the doorway at the rear of the chapel, and I turned back into the aisle and hurried with my cup to my own place in the very last row. After the chapel exercises I avoided her, hiding in the locker room until it was time for classes to begin again. I was miserable, and during the afternoon I tried to forget myself in the classwork and in the games afterward. By the end of the day I was so tired that I fell asleep on the Special, and when I woke up, the streetcar was already in town. I remained completely quiet until the car had reached my own stop. Then all of a sudden I felt that I was not miserable, that I had never been so happy, that my happiness belonged to me alone and was not connected with anything else that had ever happened to me. I jumped up on the seat nearest the door and shouted, 'I have an announcement to make! Everybody listen! Monday, Tuesday, and Wednesday of next week will be followed by Thursday, Friday, and Saturday!' As I ran up the street past the drug store and into the short cut through the alley, I could hear my friends laughing, pretending to applaud, yelling my name after me. And a sort of wave of happiness swept over or through me—a sweeping feeling that was completely different from any ordinary happy feelings that I had had before. I hadn't realized that there *was* this sort of happiness or that it could ever come to me.

After Christmas my father and mother began making plans for a trip to South America. They were going to sail from New Orleans on the first of March and return to St. Louis about Easter time. Mother decided to join the girls in New York for their February holidays and to spend a week there buying clothes for her trip.

Returning to St. Louis only a week before they were supposed to leave for New Orleans, she insisted that she wished to spend her first evening at home modeling her new clothes for Father and me. So that night Father and I seated ourselves on her bed while she retired to her dressing room. Father was smoking. I sat with my mathematics book open in my lap.

Each time she appeared from her dressing room, I applauded. If she appeared in a dress that I liked especially, I stamped my feet. But my father, I observed, seemed generally apathetic to the whole performance and at times so inattentive that I felt compelled to draw his attention, saying, 'How do you like this one?' Mother's high spirits and her interest in the new clothes seemed to blind her to his mood of indifference. Before each appearance she would call out some newspaper phrase to describe her ensemble: 'A smartly tailored gabardine!' or 'White bouclé with accessories of green.' Then she would enter, walking unsteadily as though on shipboard. And finally when she appeared wearing a flannel suit and carrying a bright plaid blanket under her arm, she paused before her husband and asked, 'Can you direct me to the promenade deck, sir?'

Father leaned toward the bedside table and dropped his cigarette in a glass of water there. 'Ann, dear,' he said with unnatural calm, 'I have some bad news.'

'What on earth, Gerald?'

'We can't take this trip.' He spoke with such quiet calm and with so little concern in the tone of his voice that my stepmother, who had not perceived his abstraction tonight, immediately supposed it was all a joke.

'Don't tease me, Gerald.'

Father's eyes roved aimlessly over the furnishings of the room. 'Last Wednesday afternoon,' he said, 'the board of directors finally asked for my resignation.'

'Why, how could they?' She spoke as though she were being accused. 'They would have to give you more consideration. You're no mere wage-earner to be laid off with Saturday's pay.'

'No, not just exactly. I'll be given six months' salary and be called in 'for advice' during that period.' Now he smiled rather condescendingly at her, and it was that smile that brought home to me how little my rich stepmother knew of modern business. 'An executive's position is not so strong as it was in your father's day,' Father told her.

The same smile seemed to convince Mother that the news, which had been incredible a few minutes before, was undoubtedly true. For a moment she stood there with her lips slightly parted and her eyes focused on the toe of Father's brown shoe; then her eyes flashed upward and met Father's eyes, about which there was an unnatural calm and steadiness. 'And why have you chosen this moment to tell me?'

she asked. Now she quickly snatched the little beret from her head. 'Why didn't you tell me when I stepped off the train? Why didn't you tell me at dinner? Why, pray, have you sat there watching me make such a fool of myself?'

I looked back and forth from Mother to Father, trying not to hear what they were saying, trying not to think anything about anything.

'Several members of the board deliberately deceived me when I went to them in December.' His eyes seemed to take no account of her gaze; they were roving again now in a slow, measured movement over the objects in the room.

'You've let me parade about in these garments,' she said, 'knowing all the while the trip was definitely out.'

His eyes seemed to catch on some point in the far corner of the room and then cut sharply toward her. His head didn't move; it was only his eyes. 'Do you hear what I'm saying to you, Ann?'

'First, I want to know what depraved pleasure you can take in seeing me so ridiculous?'

'*You* so ridiculous?' He rose to his feet, and she backed away toward the door to her dressing room as though it were an exit to the hall and as though she were leaving the scene. She disappeared for a moment and then reappeared with several of the new dresses thrown over each arm. 'You have sat there estimating the price of each of these. You could not be satisfied until you had humiliated me before Quint, made me appear extravagant and fatuous in his eyes.'

'On the contrary, Ann,' he said amicably now, 'my intention was to ask you to be so extravagant as to pay for our trip yourself.'

'I?' One strand of hair, which had come loose when she jerked off the beret, now fell down on her shoulder. 'Pay for the trip that you conceived to make amends for your dreadful behavior at Christmas?'

My father blushed. 'Amends? I have never felt the need to make amends to you for anything. You are a spoiled rich woman.' At first he started toward the closet—probably he could not have said why—and then turned and went out through the doorway to the hall. Mother stared at me intently for several minutes; then she motioned for me to go away.

The next night there was a rehearsal of the musical comedy at school. I did not come home until after ten o'clock. As I opened the front door, I realized that during the entire day the trouble between my parents had not once entered my mind, and although I was shocked at my own callousness, I was even more concerned over the state in which I might find affairs tonight. I looked into the library. Father was seated at the desk.

'Come in, Quint.'

I ambled into the room and fell into one of the heavy, cushioned chairs. I slumped down into the corner of the chair and exhaled one long, audible breath which was to indicate that the life of a musical comedy star was no easy one and that I hoped he would not burden me with confidential talk tonight. 'What is it, Father?'

'Quint, things are in a right bad shape.'

'Business things?'

'You know quite well what I mean, son. Sit up in your chair, Quint.'

I straightened myself, and I did not resent my father's tone; I knew I should be ashamed of my own indifferent manner. I knew that I ought to have come in and said something to him about his and Mother's misunderstandings and to have tried in some way to help them understand each other. Finally I said, 'Father, what's the matter with you and Mother?'

Several times he seemed to be preparing to explain. His lips would move, and then he would lift his eyebrows as though a new thought had occurred to him. At last he managed to say, 'I can't put my finger on where our differences began any more than I can say where my differences with the board of directors began.'

I dropped my eyes to the carpet.

'That's not a very satisfactory answer, I guess.'

'No, sir.'

'Your mother thinks—'

I raised my eyes to his.

'Your mother will tell you what she thinks, I suppose.'

'Yes, sir.'

'Your mother mistakes the significance of many things I say and do, Quint. Last night I tried to make it appear that I cared little for having lost the best job I'll ever have. I had thought that would please her. You saw how disastrous the result was. The truth is, Quint, your mother sets great store by money—in a sense that you and I may not understand. Do you know what I mean?'

'No, sir.'

'No, you don't. And I can't explain it. But has she ever suggested to you that I married her for her money?'

'I guess so.'

'I had supposed she had, for that's been on her mind lately. And I have said that she married me only to get you. She had always wanted a son, you know.'

'But, Father, she didn't do that.'

'Your mother and I have gotten in the habit of saying kind of bad things to each other—even worse things than we say in your presence. But that's not what I want to talk to you about. I want to talk about our future—yours and mine.'

'Yes?'

'I'm going back on the road—traveling for another concern.'

'And what about me, Father?'

'I want you and your mother to find us an apartment—one that I can afford to pay for. We can't live here on your mother's charity, Quint.'

'Where is Mother?'

'She's upstairs in her room.'

'What does Mother say about this?'

'She'll have to make her choice, Quint.'

'I'll go up and see her.'

'Yes, I want you to.'

When I reached the doorway I turned and looked back at my father. 'Good night,' I said, trying to say it as though this were but another school night when I must go to my room and study. He nodded his head rather mechanically. At that moment I was convinced that he had been altogether misunderstood by Mother—and unfortunately so at the very time when he was being betrayed by his business associates.

I hurried through the hall and up the steps. Mother was waiting for me at the head of the stairs. She was dressed for bed, wrapped in a long quilted robe and wearing her hair in two plaits pinned about her head. 'How is the play going?' she asked, and she put her arm about me and walked with me to the upstairs sitting room where there was a fire burning in the big grate. I had never known a fire to be lit there before, and I asked her for the reason for it. She told me that she felt chilly tonight—as though she might be taking cold. As we seated ourselves before the fire, she remarked that they used always to keep a fire there in the wintertime when her father was alive; and for several minutes she sat talking about her papa and his temperamental dislike of steam heat. 'When we were living abroad, Papa would say the only thing he dreaded about coming home was the "damnable, soporific, universal steam heat in America." He would never have had central heating put in this house except that he knew how much I wanted it, how much I hated the drafty hallways in old-fashioned houses, and how easily I caught cold. "It's to be your house," he used to say to me, "and I'm going to build it for you in every detail."'

'Mother,' I interrupted her, 'I thought . . . I expected you to be more upset. . . . I've just been talking to Father downstairs about things.'

She looked at me curiously for a moment, as though there were no reason in the world for her to be agitated. Then, with no change in her facial expression, she said, 'Oh, anything can happen before next fall.'

'Isn't he going back on the road till then?'

'Yes, I think he is.'

'Well, Mother, . . . what do you mean?'

She bent forward and gazed indifferently at the flames above the grate. With no emotion whatsoever— without much interest even—she said, 'I mean that even he agrees that you had better finish at least this year at Country Day.'

Neither of us spoke for several minutes. At last I said, 'Oh, it's all right about that.' And when my stepmother, who was still bent forward with her elbows on her knees, looked at me over her shoulder, I read a slightly changed expression in her eyes.

'Of course it is,' she said. 'Because something will happen. I must keep this house one more year, Quint. I have to stay here until my girls have made their debut next fall. Then I'll go anywhere he wants to live.'

'Surely he'll understand that. Have you told him?'

'Oh, have I told him!' She looked quite solemn but in no sense unhappy or distraught. 'How do you think I've spent the past twenty-four hours, my boy? This afternoon I finally slept for a couple of hours.'

Under my breath, between my teeth—it must have been almost a hiss—I said, 'God-amighty.' It seemed to me then that it was my stepmother who was completely misunderstood by my father.

'He says, Quint, that it's not for the girls' sake I want to stay here but that I am intent only upon keeping you in this house and in that school. Quint, I do mean for you to stay in the school, but he won't take money from me and won't let me keep you in school.' Her bearing was still tranquil and composed, but tears had filled her eyes and were beginning to streak down her cheeks.

I felt bound to take no notice of her tears. 'Can't he do better than going back on the road?'

'Do you think he can't do better than that, Quint?' After several moments she said, 'I've asked your father to handle my own business interests, to take Mr. Curtis's place. But it seems we can't talk about money sensibly.'

'Mother, surely you know he didn't marry you because of your money.' When I said this I didn't look directly at her, and I mumbled my words.

'If he did, he doesn't remember it now.' Her tone was again completely vague and detached. 'And if I married him to get you, I don't remember it now. I used to be sure I did not.'

Her voice trailed off into a whisper, and I found my own attention wandering in a strange way to familiar objects in the sitting room. Already I had grown accustomed to the fire's burning there in the grate. When finally I spoke, it seemed to me that I was speaking my thoughts involuntarily. 'Nothing really bad is going to happen. All this will be smoothed over.' My real reason for speaking was to hear the familiar sound of my own voice in this familiar room, but I saw at once that she had taken comfort from what I said.

'Suddenly, Quint, you seem a grown man to me.' She smiled intimately, and for a moment it was like old times between us. Then, withdrawing again into her unintelligible mood of apparent serenity, she said with a faint smile: 'We're making you old before your time.'

After a while I made a move to leave, but she asked me to sit a little longer with her. We remained before the fire in silence until the clock in the hall struck eleven. Then I said again that we should go to bed; but again she begged me not to leave her just yet. Fifteen minutes later I stood up and went and kissed the top of her head where the two long plaits were coiled. The moment my lips touched the tightly plaited hair I heard her sharp intake of breath and felt her body wrench with the first sob. Then, as she burst into tears, she clasped her arms about my waist and forbade me to leave her. I stood stroking her head as tears ran freely from my own eyes.

It was midnight when I went to my room. While I had sat with my stepmother during the past hour, I had thought of myself as a man; and on the stairs just now I imagined that my footsteps sounded heavier than they had when I came up from the first floor. Inside my room, I stopped before the looking glass and perhaps for the first time took an interest in my own face. 'In six more months I'll be fourteen,' I said aloud. 'For my age, I'm tall,' I said, 'but my face is still round like a baby's.' In my exhaustion I began to dream idly of what I would do when I was sixteen and had an automobile of my own; but I could not long avoid the reality that my future was again uncertain. All of my personal happiness still seemed really contingent upon the continued happiness of our family life. I threw myself across my bed, sick at heart, full of self-pity, blaming my father for being so deceived by other business men and reproaching my mother for having once sat on this very bed and promised that things would never be different for me. I wished that I could go that instant and catch a streetcar for Country Day and spend the night on a cot in the gymnasium the way we did on Friday nights after Scout meeting. Instead I pulled a blanket over me and slept there till morning with my clothes on.

On Saturday morning, two days later, old Herman came down to my workshop in the basement and said that 'the missis' wanted me to go with Gus on an errand for her. It was an unusual sort of request to come from Mother, and I knew well enough that Herman never spoke of her as 'the missis' except when he was a little piqued about something. For a minute I didn't switch off the motor of the jig saw and kept pushing the piece of wood I was working on against the blade. I waited until Herman was gone, and then I switched it off and went up to Mother's room on the second floor.

I found her standing by one of the front windows. She was wearing the same quilted dressing robe that she had worn two nights before, but when she turned around, her face was full of color and her eyes sparkled. She wasn't smiling, but she looked happy and busy, as though she had stopped by the window only to rest a moment from some quite agreeable task. In the middle of the room a card table had been set up, and on it were pieces of brown paper, a roll of twine, and a pair of scissors. But it was only the quickest glance I gave the room; I could hardly take my eyes off Mother's face.

'Yes, I know I must look a sight,' she said, smiling. 'But I've just finished a whale of a job, Quint.' I came forward and looked about for the packages which plainly she had been wrapping. Seeing no packages, I looked at her again. 'They're not here,' she said. 'They've been taken to the car. My part of it's done, as much as I am physically capable of. And I'd have got Elsa to do *that* even,' she laughed, 'except I didn't consider it exactly in the line of duty.'

'Why not? What do you mean?' I asked.

'I guess what I mean is that I didn't consider it any

of her business.' Meanwhile, she had crossed the room and was closing the door which I had left open. Then she went back to her dressing table between the two front windows, and opening a drawer there she said, 'I'm going to give you some money to take along, Quint.' Picking up the ostrich skin wallet which I had given her for Christmas and holding it in her two hands, she said, 'Of course I haven't the remotest idea of what it will take.'

'What is it for, Mother?' I made no effort to conceal my irritation.

'You *are* willing to do this thing . . . for me?'

'What?' I said flatly.

'What?' she echoed.

'What *thing*, Mother?'

And now she laughed that familiar hearty laugh of hers that could never fail to charm me, and I laughed too. 'Why, I *haven't* told you what it's all about, have I?' she said.

'You haven't told me anything.'

'I've been so worked up about keeping it from everybody else that I forgot to tell you. I am returning all that trousseau I bought for the South American trip.'

'Well, I don't see why,' I said sharply, feeling that she was about to involve me further in hers and Father's difficulties.

'Never you mind why, Quint,' she said, as though I were a small child. 'You just do this for Mother, and we'll never talk about it. I entrust it to you, Quint. I want you, not Gus, to attend to mailing the packages. He knows what they are of course, and he'll take them into the post office for you, but you see to the actual mailing and insuring. I've marked the value on each one. Don't let Gus do anything but carry the packages. It's a very personal matter and something that no servant should have any hand in.'

I accepted the wallet from her and went down to the porte-cochere where Gus was waiting for me in Mother's limousine. The back door of the car was standing open, and Gus was already in the front seat with some of the packages piled on the seat beside him. Almost before I could get in and close the door we were rolling down the driveway into Portland Place. The glass between us was closed, and I didn't even try to talk to Gus because I knew that he had piled the packages there beside him on purpose, so that I would have to sit in the back.

Within a very few days—certainly before the next Saturday—Mother had received letters from all four of the New York stores. Three of them agreed to accept the things she had returned, stating in almost identical language that this was possible only in view of Mother's patronage over many years. But the fourth store replied that two of the dresses showed signs of having been worn and that therefore no 'settlement' could be made. Mother called me to her room after dinner on Friday night and showed me the letters. 'What would you do?' she said. 'You're the only person I can talk to about this.'

'About the two dresses they won't take back?'

'Of course, Quint!' She took the letters from me abruptly. 'Gosh, sometimes I think that even you try not to understand me.'

'*Is* there anything you can do?' I asked. 'I don't guess you would want to *make* them take back the dresses.'

'Oh, wouldn't I? And I've *got* to some way, Quint.'

I could see that she did have to, and I began trying to think of some lie that she could write them, or just anything.

'The other places didn't hesitate,' she said. 'It's that Miss King who waits on me there. She's always re- sented me—and the girls too somehow. God knows why we've kept going back to her all these years. She's one of those salespeople who instead of trying to sell you something, try to make you feel extravagant for just buying clothes to put on your back.'

'Mother,' I said, 'why don't you call Laura and Bess and ask them to go down and talk to the people at the store personally. Bess could persuade anybody to do anything.'

'Why, yes, that's the only thing to do now,' she said, as though she had already been considering it. 'I must call the girls. As a last resort I'm willing to do almost anything.'

When Mother had given the name of the girls' school to the operator she motioned to me to bring her the stool from the dressing table. I brought it, and she sat down on it instead of on the bed where she usually sat when making telephone calls. For some crazy reason I was confident that I had hit upon the real solution. I went around to the other side of the bed and lay down on the bed, on my back with my eyes closed. I felt so relieved and so exhausted that I may even have dropped off to sleep for a moment while Mother was waiting for the call to go through. At any rate, the first real awareness I had that Mother was actually talking to someone at the school came when I heard her saying, 'What do you mean they are not there this week? Aren't you having classes? Where are they?' I opened my eyes and looked at Mother without turning my head. I knew, and I was certain that she did, where Laura and Bess must be. They were off somewhere with their real father and his wife. 'I should like to know exactly where my daughters are,' Mother was saying. I closed my eyes again and I could hear the nervous voice at the other end of the wire. Presently I heard Mother put down the receiver. 'They're with their own father in Connecticut,' she said to me. 'I'm going to call them at his place up there.'

After a while I heard her say, 'Hello, Bess, dear.' It was not the voice I had been hearing for the past two weeks. It was Mother's *real* voice, casual and gay. It made me feel good. I opened my eyes and looked at the ceiling. 'Of course I'm all right, dear. No, no, nothing's the matter; I'm sorry if I gave you a scare. . . . Hello, Laura, darling. . . . I want one of you to do an errand for me. . . . An errand, I said, when you go back to New York.' And in the same voice she told them about the two dresses, not mentioning all the things

she had returned to the other stores, not even mentioning that she and Father were not going on the trip.
I heard her telling them about her letter to the store
and about what the store had replied. Then I heard her
telling it all over again. I believe she went over the
whole thing three times, and each time in that same
voice, as though it were not really so important to her.
Laura and Bess must have taken turns at listening, or
maybe one of them had gotten on an extension. Neither of them must have said anything for a while, because when Bess did speak I could hear her very
clearly.

'You'd better count me out, Mother-chum,' she
said. 'Let old Laura do it. She's the girl with guts.'

'I'm serious about this, Bess,' Mother said.

Then I heard Laura say, 'Let George do it.' And the
girls began laughing.

'Be serious, for once,' Mother said.

'Not me,' said Bess. 'Life's too short to be rowing
over two silly old dresses, Mother.'

'I'm not talking to you now, Bess. I'm talking to
Laura. Will you do it, Laura?'

'Stick my neck out, Mother? For that old hatchet-
face Miss King to chop off?'

'Will you do it?' Mother said.

Both Laura and Bess seemed to be choking with
laughter. Suddenly I got up and hurried around the
end of the bed. I was going to take the telephone from
Mother and tell them that this was important to her.
One of the girls was saying something as I got up; by

the time I had rounded the end of the bed I could see that Mother was about to put down the receiver. I stopped several feet away from her, but I could hear the man's voice that came over the wire. 'Ann, honey, this is me,' he said. Mother put down the receiver.

In that instant a ridiculous question flashed across my mind: If I had taken the telephone just as he came on the wire, how should I have addressed Mr. Lauterbach? Other, even more ridiculous questions might have occurred to me, except that I hastened to find something else to think about. Quickly I began trying to prepare myself for what I expected to be the worst scene of all with Mother. But she only got up and moved the stool back to the dressing table. When she turned her face to me again she looked pale, but her voice sounded very much as it had on the telephone. 'I guess there's not much we can do about my old problems, Quint. How about yours? Have you gotten up your lessons for tomorrow?'

'Tomorrow's Saturday,' I said.

'Then why aren't you at the movies?' she smiled. She came over and kissed me and said she wouldn't have *anything* standing in the way of my Friday night movie.

During the first week in March Father moved all his papers from his office to the house in Portland Place. He spent several days sorting these papers, some of which he packed in wooden crates and sent to the basement for storage. Others he kept in the library until the following week, when he took up the duties of his new job. During this interval I had no private interview with either of my parents, and I avoided sitting with them after dinner in the evenings. Although I could perceive that they observed my efforts to avoid them, still I could not keep myself from trying to spend as little time as possible with them. If there were a night rehearsal of the musical comedy, I stayed for it even though my scenes were not being rehearsed. That week end I went to four picture shows.

Every morning I would try to leave for school without saying good-by, but Mother never failed to catch me on the stairs or at the front door. She would kiss me gently and then gaze questioningly into my eyes and say, 'I don't see you any more, Quint.' At night sometimes she would come to my room, but as soon as I heard her footstep I would switch off the light and pretend to be asleep. Then I would lie awake in the dark, longing to talk to her and have her tell me that something would happen to straighten matters out. One night I heard my father on the stairs. I waited until his footsteps sounded clearly in the hall before I snapped off the switch, knowing that he would actually see the light go out. The footsteps stopped a moment and then began again. In the doorway my father's figure was just an outline against the dim light from the hall. When he said, 'Quint!' I didn't answer; from my bed I watched him pausing there, then turning quickly to go down the long hallway to the stairs. As I settled my head on the pillow, I felt a nervous twitching at the corner of my mouth and I put my hand up to stop it. It seemed that the outside world which had once been so hostile and strange was now my very own and that my parents were becoming strangers to me.

Soon Father was much occupied with his new work. Dinner had to be kept waiting for him in the evening sometimes; often he would have left the house before I did in the morning. But conversation at mealtime was not so strained as it had been for a while. Father talked about his new employer and the other salesmen just as he had once talked about the executives with whom he had been associated. Yet when Mother suggested once that he invite some of his new associates to dinner, he answered that that would not be at all necessary, and left off talking for the remainder of that meal. I observed that he no longer wore the tailored suits that I was accustomed to, but usually dressed in one of his old ready-made business suits that he had Mother bring down from the attic. And he frequently expressed disapproval of the expensive clothes which some of the other salesmen wore. 'Mighty poor judgment,' he said. 'Far beyond their means.' He also criticized them for not showing proper respect for the executives in their company. Particularly offensive he found one salesman who liked to say, 'Gerald Dudley should be in there making the decisions; he knows more about running the show than those big boys.'

'Well, probably you do, Gerald,' Mother said.

'Now, let's understand this,' he replied, putting down his knife and fork and resting his hands on the table. 'If I were the good executive Mr. Reese or Mr. Beerman or Mr. Waymeyer is, I'd still be in an executive position.'

There had been a time when Mother would have laughed at the way he listed those names, but she no longer made light of Father's pronouncements; and she didn't tease him in any way. Yet neither did she seem frustrated or depressed by his dourness and apparent perversity. She listened to him, and she kept her eyes on me; but, except during those moments when she clasped me to her on the stairs or at the front door, she still had the detached and vague manner which I had first noticed that night in the sitting room before the fire.

Coming in from school one evening, I glanced into the dining room and saw only two places set at the table. Before I had got out of my overcoat, Mother appeared on the stairway; and as she descended she began telling me that my father had left today for his first tour of duty. 'He has gone to Kentucky and Tennessee and won't be back until a week from Saturday. He told me to tell you to take good care of me.' At dinner we gossiped about the day's happenings, and afterward we went to the library for a game of cards. That evening I felt I was enjoying my mother's company as I used to do; but on the next evening and on those that followed during the ten days my father was away, I became increasingly self-conscious in her presence and often felt that I was being detained in the library against my will. I soon came to dread the evening meal and the game of cards. More than the evenings, however, I came to dread those late afternoons when Mother drove out to school for me in her limousine. When the last bell rang and the final study hall was dismissed, I would rush out of the building and down the cinder path toward the trolley line; and I would sometimes be in sight of the Special before I recognized the insistent blowing of her automobile horn, which I had tried so hard not to hear. One afternoon I had even got aboard the streetcar when I saw Gus, dressed in his soft-gray uniform, racing down the path waving his cap and trying to call out to me above the noise the other boys were making. I sat quietly by the window, waiting to see whether or not the streetcar would move off before my stepmother's chauffeur reached me. Only after it was apparent that Gus would positively win the race did I alight from the Special and go forward to join him. As we walked up the path toward the parking lot, I tried to make conversation about the Cardinals and the Browns and about Charles A. Lindbergh, who was planning to fly the Atlantic in his plane called *The Spirit of St. Louis*.

My stepmother greeted me as usual, never asking me why I did not look to see if she were waiting in her car. Then I began to dread the inevitable turn that the conversation would take:

'Quint, I sometimes wonder . . .'

'Yes?'

'. . . how I ever got along before I had a boy of my own.'

'Oh, you had the girls home then.'

'I often think that you're closer to me than most boys are to their mothers.'

'You bet I am,' I would say with a wink. But she did not respond to my gaiety nowadays.

'I like to hear you say that. When you're older, you'll understand how it is.'

The night my father returned, I was called in to receive messages from my grandmother, whom he had seen in Tennessee. As always, Mother expressed great interest in Grandma Lovell. 'I do wish you would ask her to come to visit us, Gerald. She must be sick for the sight of Quint.' We were in the library waiting for dinner to be announced.

'Yes, I'd not realized how much she would want to see him. She has a score of other grandchildren, you know.'

'We *must* get her to come to see us.'

'She even asked me what games you like, Quint, and whether or not you liked to read. I was ashamed I couldn't tell her much about what you like.'

'Shall I write to her, Gerald,' Mother said eagerly, 'and ask her to come?'

'No, I think not. She has aged mightily, and I don't believe she would want to make the trip. I think Quint had better pay her a visit this summer.' Then he turned to me. 'What do you think of spending the summer with Grandma, like old times?'

I saw Mother wince. 'No, Gerald,' she said. 'We're going to Michigan.'

Without looking at her, he spoke her name. Then after a moment's hesitation, with his eyes still on me, he said, 'Ann, the boy can't spend this summer in a resort. If he don't go to his grandma's farm, he is old enough to get some little job to occupy him in St. Louis. He's got to learn to shift for himself.'

My stepmother got up from her chair and stood with her feet set wide apart. 'Gerald, you're deter- mined to take him from me!'

At that moment old Herman drew back the por- tieres and announced dinner. But Mother turned and passed through the doorway into the hall. And then in another instant Father and I had hurried after her, for we had heard the strange, fuzzy sound of her voice when she gasped and then the thud when she fell forward on the carpet. Father called out, 'Fetch us some water, Herman,' and Herman was at his mistress's side almost as soon as her husband and son.

She was revived in only a moment, but Father would not allow her to move. He sent Herman scurrying up the steps for a blanket. I sat beside her on the floor, holding her hand, while my father knelt at her other side, holding the damp napkin in place on her forehead.

'I'm afraid you're a sick girl,' Father said tenderly.

'You're darned right I'm sick,' she whispered, smiling; and she motioned for him to remove the napkin.

'We're going to get a doctor here right away, darling.'

'Oh, no, we're not,' she said, and her voice resumed some of its ironic, poised quality. 'I've *seen* a doctor. My husband, I'm going to have a baby. I've been pregnant for three months,' she said, 'and I'm not going to have a fool doctor in this house tonight. They won't admit I'm pregnant.'

I thought I felt her hand moisten as she spoke, and my own body was presently drenched in perspiration. As I stared at my mother and father, my mind seemed to detach itself from the scene in order to try to comprehend the new situation; and all of my faculties were so out of focus that my father's voice sounded small and indistinct, and I felt that I was looking at both Father and Mother through the wrong end of Mother's opera glasses. My mind was floundering desperately, grasping at every straw of information

127

that I could recall concerning sex and pregnancy and childbirth. I was remembering certain books I had browsed through and various details given me by older boys at school and even a sensational newspaper account of a woman who gave birth to a child while alone in the woods. Then suddenly my mother cried out in a voice muffled and remote: 'By God, no! By God, no!' At first her voice was remote, but it grew loud and real as simultaneously she and Father once again assumed their normal proportions in my eyes. 'You bring one of those wicked fakers here, and I'll leave this house with my baby.' In another moment she had forced herself up from the floor, turned first toward the stairway, then back to her husband, and with a frantic gesture had thrown her arms about his neck. While she wept there, I took the blanket from Herman and wrapped it awkwardly about her.

After Father had taken her upstairs, I sat on the bottom step thinking of my stepmother. An open hatred of my father flared up within me and so consumed my reason that I once rose to my feet with clenched fists. I turned my face upward in the direction of their room. What right had my father to be with her now? There was no knowing what further pain he might inflict upon her. But as I stood thus at the foot of the great twisting stairs, I found myself becoming painfully conscious of the significance of their sharing a room together, of their private relationship which excluded the whole world, and I became most perplexingly aware of my own ignorance and of my real incredulity concerning the act of love between husband and wife. Then suddenly, through this awareness, with the thought of the baby that was to be born here, I felt that I was able to know and believe a great deal more than I ever had before; I began to suspect that during the past two years my parents' happiness and unhappiness had been greater than my own. When we had been happy in this house, it had been of their making. Our happiness had really belonged to them. But so had our unhappiness; they were responsible for that too. It had been their decision to try to make a family of us; but it seemed to me that there had been merely an illusion of a family here, an illusion that had been completely destroyed a long time ago. And if there had not been a real family, then how could there have been a real family happiness? Yet now there was to be a baby, which meant perhaps that now there was to be a family. When I sat down again I was trembling.

Half an hour later Father came downstairs. He followed me into the library where the portieres were still drawn back for dinner. 'We must have a bite of supper, I suppose, Quint,' he said.

'May I see Mother a minute?' I asked.

'You had better wait till later,' he said. He made no move toward going in to dinner. Instead, he sat down on a chair by the window and, drawing back the drapery, peered out into the street.

'You're not getting a doctor, Father!'

He turned slowly around to me. 'A trained nurse now, Quint. The doctor later.'

'Did Mother agree to that?'

'No, she did not, Quint.'

'For God's sake, Father! You two are driving each other crazy. You ought to consider Mother's feelings.'

'We must all consider her feelings in everything we do and say now. Her nerves are in a terrible condition.' He allowed the drapery to fall to and folded his hands over his knee. 'Quint, son, she's mistaken about the baby.'

'I don't believe it.'

My father kept his eyes fixed on me, and his hands remained clasped tightly on his knee. 'I know it's hard for you to believe, Quint.' He continued to look at me, but I could see that there was no concern for my feelings in his eyes and no concern about how these events would affect my life. I realized then that at some point I had ceased to be the center of his whole existence; at some point I had truly become, with the consent of all parties, my stepmother's son. Father had chosen me now simply as an object at which to stare and as a willing listener while he waited for the nurse and the doctor to arrive. 'She tells me that she has seen three doctors during the past week, and I've called one of them on the telephone.' He paused a moment and then said warningly, 'Your mother's nerves are in an awful shape, Quint. You must realize that, the sooner the better.'

'May I see her tonight, Father?'

'In the morning, Quint.'

Later I went into the dining room alone and, though I kept saying that I was not hungry, I ate gluttonously of the steak and turnip greens which had been prepared in honor of Father's return. While I was eating, the nurse arrived. I watched her talking to Father in the hall, but all I heard her say was that she had not had her supper. Still later I heard Dr. Harrison's voice in the hall, heard him saying that he had been delayed because he had had company for dinner this evening. I was now resigned to the doctor's being called in, and I followed my father and Dr. Harrison back to the billiard room where the two maids and the cook had been summoned for an interview. It was revealed that all three of the servant women had been confided in by their mistress and that all three had believed that she was really with child. 'She took on about it so tiresomely,' the cook said, 'that it did make me suspicion sometime. But she said that was why her boat trip was called off, and so that seemed natural enough.' I observed that as each of the women spoke, she first wiped her mouth with the napkin brought along from her own interrupted dinner. Before going to bed, I went into the lavatory under the landing; I thought I was going to vomit my dinner. But somehow I wasn't able to vomit. I only gagged.

In bed, I fell almost immediately into a deep slumber. But early in the evening, while the light was still on in the hall, I awoke from a dream in which I was looking at a picture of a fetus, a picture I had actually seen in a book at Dick Morrison's house. Later in the night when all the lights were out I awoke again, this time from a nightmare. I had dreamed I was the baby inside my stepmother; when I awoke I was lying curled up at the foot of my bed with my knees almost touching my chin. I got up and went to the bathroom, and this time I was able to vomit.

Laura and Bess were in the house during the last three weeks before their mother was taken to a sanitarium. When they had first arrived, they insisted that they would never under any circumstances consent to her commitment to any sort of institution. They busied themselves preparing her meals and attending her from morning till night. In addition, three nurses were retained, so that there was always someone to watch over the patient. From the beginning, I was permitted to see her only once a day, usually in the evening after dinner.

During my first visits with her she seemed at times quite herself, except that she never failed to make veiled references to her imagined pregnancy. With each succeeding visit she was inclined to talk more and more of the baby she was expecting and of the plans she was making for its education. 'The nurse says it will be a boy,' she told me once, 'though I don't know how she knows.' To the nurse she had then given her characteristic, teasing laugh and had nodded coyly. Another time she said to me, 'If it's a boy, Quint,

I'm going to name him for you, though of course his surname must be Lauterbach.' As the weeks passed, however, I noticed that it was only when talking of the baby that she really seemed at all coherent. When speaking of other things she rarely completed a sentence and was often uncertain of her own whereabouts or to whom she was speaking. She conceived the notion that Laura and Bess were traveling in Italy, and would try to give me accounts of letters she had had from them in Milan, Florence, and Pisa. Even after the girls came out from New York, their mother continued to talk of their travels, and sometimes when one of them entered the room Mother would throw her arms about her neck and welcome her home from Europe. 'St. Louis is not such a bad place, after all. One has one's family and one's position, regardless of money. But you don't like your mama's having a baby, do you? Now, tell me the truth. You're ashamed of it, aren't you?' In the same way she would sometimes call me to her and say, 'Quint, you're ashamed of your poor old mother, aren't you? You don't think it's nice for her to have two husbands, do you? And now this baby! You think I'm awful.'

At the end of the second week after the girls' arrival, they changed their minds about her being removed to a sanitarium. I had noticed their previous unwillingness even to discuss their mother's condition with Father. They had listened rather impatiently to what he said about her anxiety over his business and over a possible separation from me, and then one of them had always quoted some phrase of Dr. Harrison's. 'Dr. Harrison says her breakdown is due to a variety of things.' Or: 'It possibly goes back to something in her childhood.' Or: 'Dr. Harrison thinks it's due mainly to her time of life. He says she's always been more highly strung than most of us realized.' They never expressed any opinion of their own; they always quoted the doctor. Then it was at breakfast one morning that they began quoting Mr. Curtis, the administrator of their mother's business, instead of the doctor.

'Father, Mr. Curtis feels,' Laura had begun, 'that the sensible thing for us to do is to give up this house.'

Father seemed to be waiting for her to say more. After a few minutes of silence had elapsed, he asked, 'Do you mean get a smaller house?'

'No. Mr. Curtis feels that if Mother is not going to get any better—and Dr. Harrison says she won't—we should go back to school.'

Father said nothing. During the past month—ever since the evening he had sat waiting for the nurse and doctor to arrive—he had appeared always to be waiting for something final to happen. And now he sat at the head of the table with his back to the sunlight that poured in through the conservatory windows, waiting for his stepdaughters to announce their plans.

'Mother will be every bit as comfortable in a sanitarium. Mr. Curtis suggests that we take her to one up East, where there are more specialists and where we can see her regularly.' Bess said this quite casually as she was rising from the table. She crossed the room and passed through the swinging door into the pantry to get her mother's breakfast tray. When she had gone, Laura turned to Father and said:

'Now let me give you the real news.' She was smiling and spoke in her most familiar manner. 'Bess is planning to get married this summer. To a jazz band leader named Jerry Torrence—a band leader, mind you, for all her snobbishness.'

Father's face registered no surprise or emotion, but he said, 'If that's what's in her head, I had better have a talk with Bess. Did she know you were going to tell me, Laura?'

'Yes, indeed. She asked me to tell you, but I wouldn't discuss it with her, Father. There's no stopping her, and this Jerry's quite a nice fellow. He's a friend of our own papa's, and a favorite of his. But don't you think it's remarkable that Bess, of all people, should marry a band leader?'

'Remarkable,' Father said. Again he seemed to be waiting; and when Laura spoke again it was to quote what Mr. Curtis said about disposing of the house. Nobody, it seemed, wanted a house like this one any more. The smoke in St. Louis was so awful nowadays, and everybody wanted to live out near the Country Club grounds. So, to avoid taxes, the best thing to do was to have the house torn down and its components sold at auction. That was the way you could get the most money out of these old places.

From that day forward it seemed that almost every word and action of every member of the household was directed toward the disposal of the furniture and all the valuable objects that the girls' grandpapa had brought back from Italy. Toward the end of May I saw my stepmother for the last time. It was the morning before they took her away to the sanitarium in Connecticut, and I went in to see her before leaving for school. At first she wept and told me that she was afraid the baby might be a girl. Then, drying her tears, she told me that she thought she had a piece of soot in her eye and asked me to remove it with the corner of her handkerchief. As I took the handkerchief and drew near to her, I found that I was looking into a face that bore only the slightest resemblance to the face I had once found so beautiful. There were deep vertical lines in her colorless cheeks, and her mouth, a peculiar dull purple, drooped in the left corner so decidedly that it was moist with saliva. Her eyes appeared to have been circled with gray crayon, and from their depths she peered at me as though I were a blinding beam of light. When I leaned forward and rested my left hand on the pillow beside her, I saw the nurse, who was sitting near by, come quickly to her feet. And in the next instant the poor creature I called Mother had seized my wrist with one hand and with the other dealt me three stinging slaps upon the cheek. 'You deceitful little wretch,' she cried, 'you're plotting with the rest of them to smother my baby! And *you're* after my money too!' The nurse moved so rapidly and quietly to intervene that I was hardly aware of any struggle. A moment later I was standing at the foot of

Mother's bed, and as I watched her lying there with her head resting on the white pillow, her gray eyelids closed, her distorted mouth uttering soundless words, I tried to find the grief in my heart that I felt should be there. Presently I left her room and went into the sitting room. I threw myself into the big chair before the fireless grate, and leaning on the chair arm, I wept on my shirtsleeve, in the crook of my arm; but I knew that it was only terrible shock that made me cry. In a little while I washed my face and went downstairs.

When I came down into the big front hall that morning, Gus was leaning over the console table with the morning paper spread out before him. He looked up at me with a proud grin on his face and announced that Charles A. Lindbergh had successfully completed his solo flight from New York to Paris. As I hastened down the steps and across the hall, Gus turned back to the front page of the paper to show me the headlines. 'I knew he would make it!' I said. 'I knew he would.'

I took the paper from Gus and went into the library to read every word of the long account. While I read, my mind kept wandering to thoughts of moving into a boarding house with my father, of working in the stockrooms of the hardware company this summer, of entering the public school next fall; and I was not unhappy about my future. I stopped reading for a moment and sat gazing wide-eyed at the raisin-colored carpet. For several days I had been wondering if I should not go back to live with my grandmother on the farm. But that scheme struck me now as being fantastic; it seemed to make about as much sense as some plan for me to go with my insane stepmother to live at the sanitarium. I felt that I could not even imagine what it would be like to go back for a visit to Grandma. Instead, I suddenly had a clear image of myself as an independent stranger pushing through vast throngs of people. After a moment I took up the newspaper again and continued to read the account of the amazing solo flight and of the wild crowds that welcomed the hero at the Paris airdrome.

I read the account through again and again. Then I went back through it picking out the facts that I wanted to remember: 'The plane was in the air a total of thirty-three and one-half hours. . . . At 10:27, Paris time, *The Spirit of St. Louis* landed. . . . It was estimated that a mob of 100,000 were waiting to greet the American.' I wanted to remember those facts because they seemed important, but when I had fixed them in my mind I wasn't content. And I couldn't put down the paper until I had searched through the main story again and read one more time the paragraph that had given me the biggest thrill of all: 'His cap off, his famous locks falling in disarray around his eyes, "Lucky Lindy" sat peering out over the rim of the little cockpit of his machine. "*Cette fois, ça va!*" the Frenchmen cried. Captain Lindbergh answered, "Well, I made it." Twenty hands reached for him and lifted him out as if he were a baby. One hundred thousand Frenchmen were waiting to take him to their hearts.'

Finally I raised my eyes from the newspaper, and between the portieres I could see beyond the dark furnishings of the dining room into the bright little conservatory where Bess and my father were in conversation. I had not heard their voices at all until I saw them; yet after seeing them I could hear every word they were saying.

'Blame?' Bess was saying. 'Of course there is blame. But what good would it do to point out where it lies?' Her back was almost turned to Father. They evidently had been talking there for some time, possibly about Bess's marriage to the band leader, and Bess had been on the point of leaving when Father had introduced a new subject that brought this reply from her. She was looking at him over her shoulder when she spoke. He hesitated, and even from where I sat I could see that his face was getting red.

'If I'm to be blamed, I would like to know it,' he said finally.

'Poor Father,' she said, half in exasperation, half in sympathy, 'Poor *man*.' Then she turned, facing him again, and I could hear her heels scrape on the tile floor of the conservatory. Neither of them spoke for a time. At last she said, 'Of course, nobody's really to blame. It's only the circumstances, and this dreadful life here in St. Louis.'

'But I can't believe,' Father said, 'that anything in the quiet, easy life she lived could work such a change in anyone.'

'Oh, have it your own way then!' Bess shouted at him. 'You're to blame! And my own father's to blame! And her own dear papa was to blame! And—' She was now striding through the dining room and her eyes fell briefly on me as I sat folding the morning paper and gazing dumbly at the scene before me. '—And *he, he!*' she said under her breath.

I sprang from my chair and answered her. 'No, Bess, you're the one. You and Laura. And Mother, she was wrong, herself!' Then it was, when I had expressed this resentment against my stepmother, that genuine tears first came to my eyes.

'There!' Bess said, 'I've been expecting that.'

Through my tears I saw Bess going up the stairs in the hall, and I turned and saw that Father had sat down on one of the little iron chairs in the conservatory. In his bewilderment he sat staring at the breakfast table which was set for the four of us. At that moment I was struck by the thought that he was still a very young-looking man, that there were still no gray hairs in his head of thick black hair, that he was the same man who had come for me in a taxi long ago at my grandmother's farm. I went back into the library, and seeing the morning paper which had fallen to the floor, I read over the headlines again. And when I read the headlines I was overcome with grief for my stepmother; standing in the center of the room, without even putting my hands to my face, I wept bitterly, aloud.